ALEX NEPTUNE

◄─MONSTER AVENGER─►

DAVID OWEN

USBORNE

CONTENTS

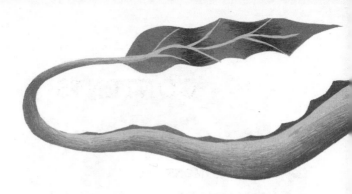

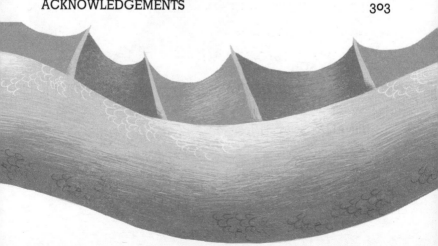

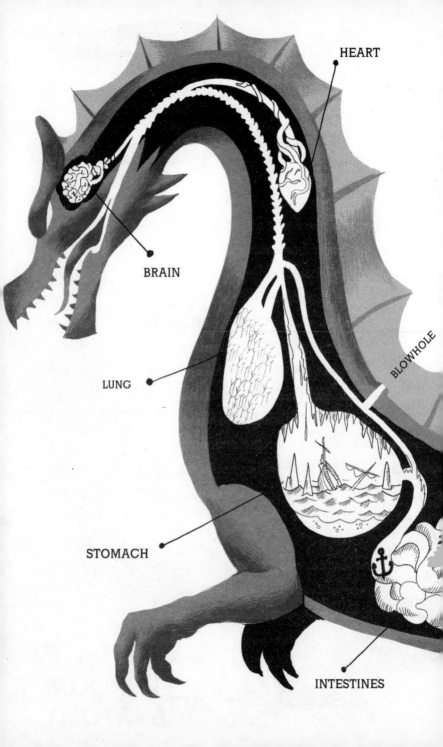

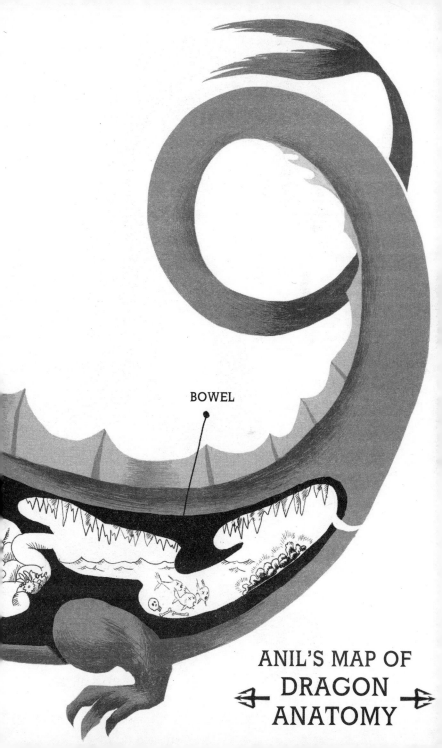

CHAPTER ONE

SHIPWRECK SEASON

It was probably a bad idea to try and capture an angry seal in the middle of a storm.

A gust of wind swirled off the tempestuous sea and lashed Alex Neptune with stinging rain. He crouched on the slick rocks of the breakwater that cleaved through the beach, stiff fingers pressing binoculars to his eyes.

Through their shaky view, Alex watched Loaf, a hefty harbour seal who lived in the usually calm waters of Haven Bay, growling at seagulls around the far curve of the bay. The blustery weather didn't seem to bother him at all.

"There's rain in my armpits!"

The storm certainly *did* bother Zoey Wu, huddling at the foot of the breakwater to put the finishing touches to a contraption set into a shallow dip in the sodden sand. Tired of enduring wet underwear every time they visited the beach, Alex's best friend now wore slick green fishing waders over an oil-stained T-shirt. Unfortunately, these did little to protect her upper half from the elements.

"Almost ready," Zoey called, hands moving deftly over the complicated kit.

Alex opened his mouth to respond but a squall of wind blew salty brine down his throat.

The rain had tipped down all week, the sky bruised permanently black. Torrents of water flooded the cobbled streets of the town. Vicious gales blew ashore without warning, ripping trees from their roots and even the stoutest locals off their feet.

Most troubling of all was that two fishing boats had been caught by surprise and wrecked. The lifeboat brought home the broken vessels but none of their crew. The missing fishermen had not been found, either drowned or alive, search parties forced back empty-handed by the storms. The fishing crews seemed to have simply...disappeared.

That wasn't even the strangest thing that had happened recently.

Below, Zoey scraped sand over her contraption and climbed the rocks to join Alex.

"The trap is set," she said, rain dripping from her black

fringe and beading on the streaks of oil across her cheeks. "Where's Anil?"

"Here!"

Anil Chatterjee hurried along the beach; a newspaper-wrapped bundle held over his head did nothing to stop the sideways-driving rain. He climbed up and set the soggy package on a flat rock.

"I've got the bait."

Zoey frowned. "Are we *sure* battered sausages are the best thing to feed a seal?"

"They're his favourite," said Alex. "We need to lure him this way without putting ourselves in danger."

"Any chance you can just *ask* Loaf to stop being so aggro?" said Anil.

A few months ago, Alex and his friends had discovered that the Water Dragon, mythical main character of countless stories passed through generations of their sleepy seaside town, was actually *real*. Together they had rescued the dragon from the clutches of predatory poacher Raze Callis and then stopped him from stealing its only egg.

A bond with the Water Dragon had awakened ancient sea magic in Alex. As well as giving him the power to control the ocean, he could also connect with sea animals and work alongside them as an ally in their ongoing fight to protect the sea.

Loaf had quickly become a particular friend, hanging around them like an overexcited, clumsy dog. The seal had proved particularly adept at knocking over quarrelsome pirates.

"Ever since Loaf started acting strangely, I've not been able to get through to him," Alex said, keeping the binoculars fixed on the seal.

Around a week ago, Loaf had climbed up onto Haven Bay's high street and raided the Chipping Forecast chip shop, drinking a vat of liquid batter and gulping down all the fish, sausages and pickled onions. When Mr Yardarm, the chip shop owner, had tried to chase Loaf away, the seal almost attacked him. Nobody – not even Alex – had been able to go near Loaf since without him growling and threatening to charge.

More sea animals who called Haven Bay their home had started behaving aggressively too. Dolphins deliberately capsized kayakers; jellyfish swarmed to sting swimmers seeking a cold dip; lobsters skittered to pinch unsuspecting toes.

Whenever Alex used his power to reach out to them, he found he was cut off. It was like a thread between them had been severed. It was a peculiarly lonely feeling, as if pieces of himself were missing.

A push from inside Alex's jacket was too insistent

to ignore. Reluctantly, he opened the zip. Octopus arms squirmed out and a splotchy blue body heaved onto his shoulder. Kraken lifted her orb-like eyes to relish the patter of cold rain.

"Don't go anywhere near the water," Alex told her, for probably the millionth time that week. "It isn't safe."

It was still only a gut feeling, but Alex was increasingly sure that something rotten had contaminated the ocean. This time it wasn't litter or chemicals clogging the waves of Haven Bay. It was something that only affected the animals. Any creatures who hadn't recently gone into the water – like Kraken, who lived in a special tank in Alex's bedroom – were still behaving normally.

When Alex called on his sea magic, it seemed to *snag* on whatever was out there. Just never long enough for him to identify it. And it couldn't be a coincidence that this was happening at the same time as two boats of fishermen had mysteriously disappeared.

The Water Dragon and its newly hatched baby still hadn't returned from their tour of the world's oceans. That left it up to Alex and his friends to find out exactly what was going on.

"Right." Zoey swiped rain from her face. "We lure Loaf closer with the battered sausages and *SNAP!* He springs the trap."

The only sign of the trap now was a slight dip in the hard-packed sand.

"How does it work?" Alex asked.

"It's based on weeverfish." Zoey puffed up proudly. "They bury themselves in sand and sting anything that stumbles over them. As soon as Loaf puts pressure on the trap, a net will burst out and wrap him up tight."

"My cousin was stung by a weeverfish once," Anil said. "It made him vomit and faint at the same time."

Alex winced. "You're sure the trap won't hurt Loaf?"

"I've never been more certain of anything in my life."

"You say that about literally everything you do."

Zoey grinned winningly. "Because everything I do is brilliant."

A plume of steam was immediately extinguished by the rain as Anil unwrapped the newspaper to reveal five greasy battered sausages, like oversized fingers. Alex and Zoey eyed them hungrily, the delicious smell briefly banishing the chill of the wind. It fell to Anil – a lifelong vegetarian – to snap them out of it by lifting a thumb and forefinger to his lips and blowing a high-pitched whistle.

A seagull descended from the brooding sky, white wings beating against the wind. The bird aimed to land on Anil's shoulder before a sharp gust blew him flapping into the side of the boy's face.

"Graceful as ever, Pinch," Anil said fondly as the seagull righted himself.

Zoey narrowed her eyes. "Are we *sure* we want to trust that bird with a mouthful of battered sausages?"

After Anil had lovingly nursed the injured seagull back to health, Pinch had repaid him in snacks pilfered from innocent tourists. Anil discouraged the habit and trained the bird to collect litter, which had only confused Pinch into stealing much more valuable belongings instead.

"He's turned over a new leaf!" Anil insisted. "Now I've trained him to return people's lost property to them."

Although no doubt an admirable ambition, the seagull had a hard time distinguishing between what was lost and what was no longer wanted. An apple core properly disposed of into a bin had a good chance of landing on your head thirty seconds later.

Anil covered his hands with his sleeves and offered a pair of battered sausages to Pinch. The seagull tilted his head and clamped them firmly in his orange beak instead of immediately gulping them down whole.

"Good boy!" Anil scratched the bird's head. "Now take them to Loaf!"

Pinch spread his wings and hauled himself into the air, a flurry of wind hurrying him along. Alex lifted the binoculars to watch the seagull glide above the beach.

As soon as he was above Loaf, he opened his beak and let a sausage fly.

The greasy finger tumbled from the sky and bonked the seal on the head.

"Direct hit!" Alex reported.

Loaf wasted no time in snaffling the sausage, thick whiskers twitching as he chewed and swallowed it in seconds. No sooner had he finished than the second sausage landed in the sand a short distance ahead of him. The seal lumbered towards the delicious morsel, bringing him closer to the breakwater and the waiting trap.

"It's working!"

Alex offered the binoculars to Zoey, but Kraken wrapped them tightly in her suckered arms and tried to peer through them, even though her eyes were too far apart.

Pinch returned to be reloaded with sausages before flying out again.

"By the way," Anil said, "Mr Argosy wants to be kept updated about what we find."

Alex frowned. Erasmus Argosy lived in the crumbling manor house outside town and was a descendant of people once bonded to the Water Dragon. The old man knew all about Alex's powers and, although he had helped them stop Raze Callis from seizing the dragon egg, Alex still wasn't convinced he could be trusted.

16

"When did you even speak to him?"

"My parents invited him for dinner again." Anil wiped a drop of rain off the tip of his nose. "They don't like him being alone in that big house."

"And you told him what we're doing?" asked Zoey.

Anil looked sheepish. "He asked really nicely. Anyway, the Argosy family tracked sea magic for centuries. He has a massive archive of records and artefacts that might help us work out what's going on. Mr Argosy even said I could help him organize it. It sounds like it's messier than Zoey's workshop."

"I'd be offended but I somehow lost my shoes in there the other day," Zoey conceded.

"Just be careful what you say to him," said Alex. "I don't want him to interfere."

They watched Pinch drop the third and fourth battered sausages, luring Loaf closer and closer to the trap. The rocks provided enough cover that they wouldn't be spotted.

"Who wants to throw the last sausage?" Alex asked.

"Oh, me! I'm the best..." Anil stopped himself snatching for it. In pursuit of discovering his unique talent, Anil used to claim he was the best at everything and hope it was true. Ever since realizing his genuine skill for storytelling, he had been trying to break the bragging habit. "I mean, I'd like to throw it, please."

Loaf finished the fourth sausage, wiped a flipper across his mouth and belched loudly.

"Now!"

Anil launched the final battered sausage over the rocks. It landed perfectly in the dip of sand where the trap was concealed.

Loaf sniffed towards it hesitantly, as if growing suspicious about such an abundant battered bounty.

"Come on," Alex urged him.

Slowly, the seal shuffled forwards until he was almost on top of the trap. It would spring at any second.

A raking flurry of wind lashed across the rock. It caught Anil, still upright from his throw, by surprise and sent him tumbling onto the sand below.

Straight onto the trap.

The wet sand opened like a ravenous jaw. A thickly woven rope net tangled around Anil's body. Loaf reared up and snorted furiously, scraping his front flippers as if preparing to charge at the helpless boy.

"Oh, heck," said Zoey.

Alex rose from the rocks. "Reinforcements!"

The beach burst open at the four corners of the trap. Four sea otters shook sand from their bristling coats and sprang to form a protective barrier between Anil and the seal.

Loaf charged at the otters, not recognizing his friends, bowling them aside to clear the path to Anil. From Alex's shoulder, Kraken fired bullets of water as a distraction, but it would only buy a few seconds.

"What do we do?" asked Zoey.

Alex pressed his hands to the rocks. They were slick enough with rain and salt water to connect him to the ocean. Sea magic swelled inside him, stronger than any storm. Whatever plagued the water may have cut him off from the animals, but it couldn't stop him using his other powers.

Tendrils of seaweed wriggled from crevices in the rocks. Knotted strands and knobbly ropes twined together as they snaked across the sand. Alex wielded them like arms to snatch at the seal's flippers, but Loaf snarled and bucked loose.

"He's too strong!" shouted Zoey.

"You know how our plans usually go horribly wrong?" Alex scrambled up to stand tall on the rocks. "But somehow we win anyway, despite doing something stupid that shouldn't work?"

Zoey nodded. "Classic us."

"Let's hope our luck holds."

Alex launched himself into the air, diving over Anil's tangled head to land on Loaf's back. The seal roared its

19

displeasure and tried to thrash him away. Alex wrapped his arms around Loaf's neck and held on as tight as he could.

It's me, he told the seal, reaching for the connection between them. *We're friends.*

The bond was still there. Alex felt the current of magic that bound them together. But it was blocked – something was interfering with the signal so his message couldn't get through.

"We're doing this to help!" Alex shouted aloud.

The otters bundled to join him on Loaf's back. Their combined weight was enough to restrain him. Alex wrapped the seaweed tightly around the seal's body. Finally, Loaf admitted defeat, slumping onto the sand with a greasy burp.

"Could somebody let me out, please?" Anil asked, hands tugging at the net.

Zoey hopped down from the rocks to help.

"This might not be the point," she said, "but I hope everybody noticed that my trap totally worked."

CHAPTER TWO

MINIATURE MONSTERS

The ice cream van served as a windbreak on top of the sea wall, which unfortunately allowed Mr Ballister, Grandpa's only customer, to study the faded photos of frozen treats without being blown out to sea. Meaning he witnessed Alex, Zoey and Anil wrestling the seaweed-wrapped seal up the steps.

"I didn't know you'd started serving sushi," he said.

Alex's grandpa shut the serving window in his face and went to help.

Mr Ballister frowned as Loaf was hefted into the back of the ice cream van. "Is that the seal who *soiled* the bowling green?"

Alex winced. "It might be."

"You really shouldn't encourage them to behave so boorishly." Mr Ballister huffed, flipped up his jacket collar, and leaned into the wind as he stalked away.

Alex strained under the seal's weight. "It's not like *I'm* making them act this way."

"Now we've caught him we can figure out what *is* making it happen," said Zoey.

Together, they slid Loaf into the space between a drinks fridge and the waffle-cone holder. Grandpa groaned, back creaking ominously, before peering around the cramped space now jammed with children, otters, an octopus and a seal.

"This must be breakin' a few hygiene codes," he grumbled.

Loaf burped loudly in protest, choking the van with the stench of rotten fish and battered sausage.

Thankfully, it was only a short drive along the blustery seafront to the boatyard where Zoey lived with her parents. They handled repairs for the locals as well as dealing in scrap. The front yard was an obstacle course of twisted metal, broken wood and tangled mounds of wires. Two large sheds sheltered the remains of the two recently wrecked fishing boats, cables clinking in the wind.

After manoeuvring the ice cream van carefully around the scrap, Grandpa parked as close to the front doors as possible. The group stretched their muscles in preparation for lifting Loaf's tremendous weight again.

Zoey rolled up her sleeves. "We should have got Bridget to help."

Alex's sister was a champion weightlifter, who would probably have slung the seal over one shoulder like a shopping bag.

"All these storms have kept her too busy working with the lifeboat crew."

A combination of lifting and dragging moved Loaf out of the van and inside the boatyard's front office. The seal groused his displeasure and strained against his seaweed bindings, but they were strong enough to hold.

Mr Wu stood behind the front desk, dabbing paint onto a large canvas tipped against the wall. "What you got there?" he asked.

"Seal," Zoey replied, without stopping.

Mr Wu didn't bat an eyelid. "Don't you think you should ask for my *seal* of approval?"

"You can't have parental authority and make jokes like that. Pick one." Zoey was still moving, forcing the others to follow. "We're on important world-saving business."

Mr Wu looked to Grandpa for support, who simply shrugged, peeling away from the group to admire the painting. The otters lined up by the front door like bodyguards.

Alex had only been inside Zoey's workshop a handful of times because doing so carried significant risk of losing a limb. Half-finished inventions and random scrap littered the room, with no way of telling them apart. A shower head, draped in bicycle chains like greasy braids, dripped oil onto a basket of decapitated plastic dolls. A brightly painted merry-go-round horse lay on its side with a single metal wing jutting from its back. Balls of paper, wood shavings and nuts and bolts completely hid the floor. Grease was smeared across the closed window blinds.

In one corner, Alex spotted a heavy metal cage patched together with chain-link fencing, large enough to hold a person.

"Preparing to take prisoners?" he asked uneasily.

"It's a Faraday cage," said Zoey as they waded across the room. "It stops you getting electrocuted, which is surprisingly important around here."

"Nothing about that is surprising to me," Anil said.

A workbench provided an island amidst the mess. Zoey roughly swept it clear of books and tools. The only item she handled with care was a jam jar half-full of seafire, the glowing green liquid that would ignite into bright, harmless flames if spilled. Lastly, she cranked the bench low enough to lie Loaf comfortably on top.

"I'm sorry," Alex said, gently stroking the seal's head.

Even now, without the chaos of the beach ambush, some unseen force blocked the connection between them like a foot on a hosepipe.

Loaf groaned and gnashed his teeth. Kraken shimmied down Alex's arm and clambered over to massage the seal's side, quietening him down.

"I've been doing a lot of reading, but biology isn't really my area of expertise," said Zoey. "I wish Meri was here to help."

Meri had become part of the team after her usually peaceful family of seafaring litter-pickers had decided to turn pirate and help Raze Callis steal the Water Dragon egg. Despite betraying them once or twice, Meri had redeemed herself by helping to defeat Callis and his pirate ship cobbled together from junk. Her reward was captaincy of the rebuilt ship – *The Dragonfly* – which she swore to use to protect the ocean.

"My parents have shown me some of their doctor skills," said Anil. "I should be able to help."

It was odd to see Anil and Zoey working together without the usual playful bickering. Maybe the strange behaviour of the animals and the missing fishermen had shaken them more than Alex realized. He knew they cared about keeping Haven Bay safe just as much as he did.

Unable to use sea magic to help, Alex simply stroked

Loaf's head, hoping the seal would take some comfort despite whatever afflicted him.

As soon as they had a blood sample, Zoey took a microscope from a cupboard and lowered her head to study it.

"What. The. Heck?" Her mouth hung open as she looked up at them. "You have to see this."

Alex and Anil moved for the microscope at the same time and knocked their heads together. Alex recovered first and pressed his eye to the viewer.

At first, he saw nothing but a pinkish blur. After a few seconds his eyes adjusted and a host of wobbly red circles appeared, blue dots hovering in the middle like eyes. Blood cells, Alex guessed. There didn't seem to be anything unusual.

He was about to lift his head and ask for help when he saw the monster.

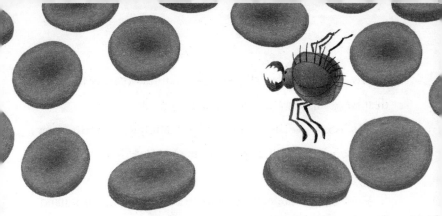

CHAPTER THREE

THE PLAGUE TIDE

Sharp, insectile legs writhed around a clear bead-like body; a bulging head was crowned with fierce, hinged mandibles. The monster propelled itself between the other cells as if they were stepping stones.

The longer Alex watched, the more of the microscopic monsters he saw. They skimmed leisurely across the blood sample and wrestled with any of their own kind they encountered.

Alex swallowed the urge to be sick. "That's probably not normal?" he said, lifting his head.

"I'm not a seal doctor, but I'm pretty sure they shouldn't be there," Zoey confirmed.

Kraken rushed towards the microscope, but Anil beat

her to it. After taking a brief look, he jumped away as if the monsters might swarm up the lens and attack him.

"It looks like some kind of parasite," Anil said. "That must be why Loaf's behaviour has changed."

"Kraken and the otters haven't been affected," Alex said. "I kept them away from the sea as soon as I sensed something was wrong. So the parasites must have come from the water."

Zoey grimaced. "What are they?"

"I might be able to answer that."

Erasmus Argosy stood in the workshop's open doorway, looking down his nose at the mess. His heavy jacket was buttoned to the neck and a chequered flat cap covered his head. Despite the wind outside, his thin white moustache still held the shape of a cat's insolent smile. The otters hung stubbornly from his arms and legs and Grandpa huffed and puffed behind him, as if they'd tried to keep Argosy out.

"The old fart's surprisingly strong," Grandpa breathed.

Argosy ignored him. "I've heard of these things before. A plague tide that takes animals as its host." He picked his way across the room and bowed to peer through the microscope. "I never knew if they were real or just...legend. They certainly haven't been seen for an extraordinarily long time."

Zoey pointed to Loaf, still wrapped up tight on her workbench. "Well, they're here now."

Once again, Alex tried to communicate with the seal. When he found the connection still blocked, he imagined the parasites clogging the thread between them, shredding his magic in their jaws. Disgust and despair swirled in his belly.

Argosy studied the seal. There was no sadness or sympathy on his face. This was simply a problem to be solved. Alex clenched his fists.

"What are you doing here?"

Argosy blinked. "Young Anil told me what you were planning. I already had my suspicions about what has been happening and I hoped you would prove me wrong. These parasites live in the ocean and infect any sea animal they encounter. They take control and make them behave aggressively to keep everything else away so that nothing can interfere."

"Interfere with what?"

"Laying their eggs. The parasites use their hosts as incubators, multiplying many times over so they can seek and infect more animals."

"I think that's the most disgusting thing I've ever heard," Zoey said.

"And we've heard a lot of disgusting things," Anil added. "Remember that time you accidentally left your walkie-talkie in the toilet and—"

Alex cut him off. He was already feeling sick. "This can't be Callis again, can it? The Water Dragon swallowed him whole."

"Nature is a much more formidable foe than any villainous pirate," Argosy said. "When the natural order becomes unbalanced, it also becomes fragile. Terrible things have a chance to thrive. The Water Dragon has done its best to sustain harmony, but without its kin, the fight is almost impossible. The dragon's need for recovery time after Callis's attack gave this foul scourge the opening it needed."

Alex had learned so much about how the well-being of the ocean impacted the entire world, how the consequences of damaging it in one place could reverberate to the other side of the planet. The less the ocean was respected, the more the world would suffer.

Still, he had never expected to be faced by an army of microscopic monsters.

"Can we stop them?" he asked.

"There's a story of a surge in infections once before." Argosy twirled his moustache as he thought. "The records say it was stopped by a Water Dragon before the parasites spread too far to be contained."

Zoey clenched her fists. "Does the record say how?"

Argosy shook his head. "The family archive has not been

properly maintained for many years. If the answer is there, we'll have our work cut out to find it."

"If the parasites can infect any sea creature," Alex said slowly, the words making him tremble as he spoke them, "could they infect the dragon?"

Zoey spun towards him in shock. Her hand knocked the jar of seafire from a nearby shelf and it crashed onto the bench, breaking open in front of Loaf. Cold green flames immediately sprang to life.

The seal thrashed as the light touched his skin, groaning and straining at his seaweed bonds as if the seafire glow dazzled him.

Anil smothered the flames with a blanket. As soon as the light was gone, Loaf settled back down into his grumbling reverie.

"You're okay." Zoey quickly checked over the seal's skin. "Seafire doesn't actually burn. You never minded it before..."

Argosy cleared his throat to regain their attention. "I don't know if the dragon would be immune."

"I have to try something." Alex hurried across the workshop, the others springing to follow him, and made his way through the front office. The otters fell into step with them.

Outside, a gale continued to snatch at their clothes, but the lashing rain had stopped for now. Alex plucked Kraken from his shoulder, her arms flailing in protest, and handed her to Zoey.

"It might not be safe for you to get this close to the water."

Then he made straight for one of the wooden jetties that pushed out into the sea. He paused at the end, toes over the edge, watching the agitated *slap-slap* of dark waves. The rest of the group stayed back to give him space.

Carefully, Alex dropped into a crouch and reached for the water. He hadn't tried to contact the Water Dragon for weeks, leaving it to the joy of guiding its newly hatched baby dragon on a tour of their aquatic territory.

A stab of long-buried fear made him freeze before his fingertips touched the water. The ominous feeling that had been bothering him for the last few days lurched inside him.

Anil seemed to read his mind. "Do you think the parasites can infect humans?"

"People have been in the water and we haven't noticed anything weird," Zoey replied. "We could do an experiment or two on you. For science, obviously."

"I think I'll pass."

"Don't worry," Argosy said. "The parasites are quite harmless to people."

Alex breathed a sigh of relief. He couldn't afford to feel scared of the ocean again. He plunged his hand into the waves.

The water was cold enough to turn his fingers numb. So when one of the countless threads that knitted the ocean together tickled his palm, he struggled to grip it at first. But then sea magic swelled inside him and he let it flow into the water.

Usually, it would zip along the thread and out into open sea like a radio signal through space. It would connect him to the Water Dragon, wherever it was, as if they were side by side. In the past, he had seen through the dragon's eyes, and heard its voice call to him in the language of the sea across impossible distances.

Now, the magic sputtered as if the current was blocked. The thread squirmed in Alex's hand, forcing him to grip it tighter. He pushed his magic as hard as he could, determined that it would make it through.

An image flashed across Alex's mind: the depths of the ocean lit by a soft green glow. He felt the familiar connection with the dragon, but tenuous, like a rope hanging from a single thread.

Pain.

The dragon was hurting. Its magic blazed vividly like it would in the middle of a fight.

Are you injured? Alex called in his mind. *Do you need help?*

The questions seemed to get strangled away before

they reached the dragon. Just like with Loaf and the other infected animals, a barrier stood between them.

Swallowing down his fear for the dragon, Alex reached out with his mind for its baby instead. Their bond had not developed yet but he was sure he could reach it. Except...

He couldn't sense the baby dragon out there at all.

The thread flexed and thrashed in Alex's hand. There was just time to hear the Water Dragon speak in the voice of the ocean: a surging current, howling wind rushing past his ears and snaps of lightning that all cried two words.

Stay away.

The pressure on their connection grew too strong. Alex tried to hold his magic firm but the thread fell away as if snipped.

The Water Dragon was gone.

"No," Alex said, head swimming, stumbling sideways as if swiped by a wave.

"Your face suggests this is going to be bad news," said Zoey.

Alex staggered upright. He felt seasick, the ground seeming to teeter under his feet like a storm-swept deck.

"I think the dragon might be—"

He was interrupted by a ringtone trilling from under Zoey's waders. She reached inside and retrieved an oversized phone.

"It's a satellite call," she said. "From Meri."

A video call window opened on the screen. It showed little more than a blur of green hair and panicked eyes as the signal faltered. Every other word was swallowed up by howling wind, crashing waves and a strange, constant *click-clack* in the background.

"...danger," Meri said. "There's something...water..."

They crowded around the screen and tried to understand.

"Are you okay?" Zoey asked.

"...chasing...baby dragon." The picture briefly cleared as Meri glanced over her shoulder in panic, before looking straight into the camera. "You have to help us."

The call disconnected. They stared at the blank screen as if Meri might magically reappear. Then Zoey growled and thumped a hand against the side of the phone.

"We can't help if we don't know what's happening!"

"Did she say they were chasing the baby dragon?" Anil asked.

Zoey tried to call back, but the phone refused to connect. Her eyes shone with worry. "Maybe. She also said she's in danger."

Alex gazed out to sea. For a moment, he felt helpless. He had been cut off from the Water Dragon and all the ocean's creatures were under threat. Meri, usually so brave, had begged for help he didn't know how to give. It was too much.

Back on his shoulder now, Kraken nuzzled close to his face, lifting an arm to rest gently on his cheek. They remained connected. It grounded him, giving him the strength he needed to stand up to everything they faced.

Before he could turn back to his friends or ask Argosy more questions, a fizzing pink light launched from further around the curve of the bay, arcing into the sky against the wind. It erupted into a shimmering pink beacon above the town. Moments later, a gust of wind carried the *boom* of the flare bursting to them.

"Not again," said Zoey.

The emergency flare lingered stubbornly on the air, defying the wind, before it faltered and faded.

The lifeboat had been summoned.

There was trouble at sea.

CHAPTER FOUR

MORE THAN A PIDDLIN' STORM

The lifeboat launched from the far side of the bay as night was falling. It skated swiftly down the rails of its launch slope and cleaved through the choppy water, lights blazing. The wind picked up the commanding throb of its engine and sent it resounding around the bay as the lifeboat accelerated towards open ocean.

From the boatyard dock, the group watched its lights grow smaller.

"I hope Bridget will be okay," said Alex. His sister had joined the lifeboat crew as a volunteer and quickly proved herself capable of joining rescue missions.

Grandpa squeezed his shoulder. "It'll take more than a piddlin' storm to stop yer sister."

"Yeah, she's pretty much the strongest person alive," Zoey said. "We should be there to help when she – I mean when *they* – come back."

"Do you think they've been called to rescue *The Dragonfly*?" Anil asked. "It sounded like Meri was in distress."

Alex hoped their friend was safe. The last crews who had called for help at sea had vanished. Somehow that had to be linked to the parasites taking over the Water Dragon and the animals. They needed to know all they could if there was any hope of making everything right.

"Whoever it is, we should be there when the lifeboat comes back," he said.

"Take a jacket." Mr Wu seemed to produce one from thin air and thrust it at his daughter.

The harbour was beside the boatyard, divided only by disused jetties in between. Zoey led them in single file along a path of the soundest boards. The wind was finally dwindling as night settled heavily, but waves still sloshed roughly around the rickety jetty struts.

Alex watched the dark water and imagined it teeming with invisible parasites – a ceaseless swarm of the miniature monsters he had seen under the microscope. There had hardly been time to think about the Water Dragon being infected. It was too terrible – too *monumental* – to consider what it might mean. How they might stop it. For now, he simply had to find out everything he could and hope for a useful lead.

He shifted Kraken to his landward shoulder, away from the water, just in case. Before the discovery of his powers, Alex would have been too scared to go this close to the ocean. Even feeling a sliver of that fear again made him feel oddly lost.

Alex turned to check on his friends and only then realized that Argosy hadn't followed them from the boatyard.

Half the town seemed to have taken the emergency flare as a summons to the harbour. The back of the main jetty was packed with people watching the sea and speculating on what might have happened.

"I heard a frenzy of sharks attacked a fishing boat and swallowed the crew whole!" said Mrs Bilge, anxiously patting the perfectly round flank of her dog Cannonball.

"That's perfectly ludicrous," Mr Ballister rebuked her. "It was a humpback whale carrying a wartime mine in its mouth that blasted the boat to smithereens."

The gossiping locals fell quiet when they noticed the arrival of Alex and his friends. A few shuffled closer together so they could continue whispering without being overheard.

Sensational rumours had been rife ever since the animals started behaving strangely. The discovery of the

Water Dragon and Alex's sea magic were an open secret in Haven Bay. He knew people speculated about what he could do, embellishing with outlandish detail. Alex had thought he preferred it that way – it had seemed safer for reality to be muddled by fiction. Now he wasn't so sure.

"It feels like everybody is looking at me," he said.

"Ignore 'em." Grandpa sneered.

Zoey had other ideas.

"If you've got something to say, you can say it to our faces!" she bellowed, digging her hands into her hips and squaring up to the crowd.

Most of them only murmured sheepishly. Slowly, Mrs Leech, who worked at the post office, was chivvied to the front against her will.

She wore a long fleece coat embroidered with wolves howling at a full moon. It stopped just short of fluffy slippers, suggesting she'd hurried out as soon as the flare went up.

"Some of us have noticed," Mrs Leech addressed Alex hesitantly, "that things were a lot more peaceful around here before you started up with your *antics*."

"My...what?" There was a sinking feeling in Alex's stomach.

Mrs Leech looked around for support. "There was no litter problem and no pirate attacks before you summoned a *dragon*." She spoke this last word as if it were both absurd and unsavoury. "Now people are going missing and the animals you brought here are causing trouble. We know you can control them..."

Alex felt as if he had been struck. "You think this is my fault?"

Nobody replied, and nobody would meet his searching gaze, which was all the answer he needed.

Immediately, Alex's eyes burned and he blinked away tears. Everything he had done was to protect the town. It broke his heart that people could think he would do anything to hurt them.

Zoey spoke before he could find any words. "Alex has risked his life to save Haven Bay, and a lot more besides!"

"Yer should be ashamed of yerselves!" added Grandpa.

Kraken curled two arms into fists and shook them at the crowd.

Mrs Bilge stepped up. Alex felt his hopes lift a little. She had been around for everything that had happened. Surely she would see the truth.

"My grandson is one of the missing fishermen," she said. "These storms aren't natural. We saw the waterspout your dragon summoned in the bay. That same power runs in your veins. How can we know what you're capable of?"

Mr Ballister nodded his agreement. "I saw you with that ruffian seal just this afternoon."

Any hope Alex had felt was dashed against the heavy

rocks that had settled in his belly. He lifted his hand to keep Zoey from shouting back. If the locals found out about the parasites, they would blame him for those too. That could interfere with finding answers.

"I know what it feels like to be scared. I don't want anybody to feel scared because of me." Alex sighed. "I tried my best to stop everything that happened."

"Maybe you could *not* try for a bit?" suggested Mrs Leech. "Keep your magic and your dragon to yourself so we can have some peace?"

"I'll show you peace," Zoey said, scuffing her feet in preparation to charge.

Any retaliation was cut short by the familiar throbbing of an engine reverberating across the water. Everybody turned to see the brightly lit lifeboat entering the bay, skipping quickly towards the harbour. This time, it wasn't towing a damaged boat behind it.

The crowd immediately began to murmur.

"Maybe they were too late."

"More fishermen disappeared off the face of the earth."

Alex swallowed his hurt. If the Water Dragon was in danger, the locals might soon see for themselves how much worse things could be. He hoped the lifeboat crew had found something that would help him get to the bottom of what was going on.

The lifeboat had drawn close enough that they could see the crew busy on deck. Bridget Neptune was twice the size of anybody else, standing with one brawny leg up on the railing as if she were a conquering captain.

"She looks so cool." Zoey sighed dreamily.

Beside Bridget, a man was wrapped in a foil blanket, hair plastered to his face and beard dripping seawater. The two previous wrecks had been found abandoned. This time, there had been somebody left behind to rescue.

The crowd rushed towards the lifeboat as it drew up to the main jetty, engine changing pitch as it slowed for Bridget to hop out and tie them up.

Alex reached her first. "Are you okay?"

Bridget grinned and flexed a burly arm. "Like, obviously."

Stopping to check on his sister meant the locals were first to reach the survivor. Alex recognized the shivering figure as a local fisherman.

"What happened out there?" Mrs Leech demanded.

"Where's the rest of your crew?" asked Mrs Bilge.

The fisherman tugged the foil blanket closer around himself, lips moving soundlessly.

"Speak up, man!" ordered Mr Ballister.

"We were attacked!" the fisherman whimpered, voice shaking.

Everybody pressed closer, waiting as the fisherman

tried to shape more words through lips almost blue with cold.

Mrs Bilge softened her voice as if she was talking to a frightened child. "Tell us what attacked you."

"The dragon," said the fisherman. "The Water Dragon sank our boat."

CHAPTER FIVE

THE WHOLE TERRIBLE TALE

The crowd broke into a cacophony of exclamations. While some demanded more information, others proclaimed they had known it all along. Zoey bellowed louder than anyone that it couldn't be true, while Anil produced a pen and notebook and started scribbling notes.

Alex took advantage of the clamour to question the fisherman. "Is the Water Dragon okay?"

"That beast is still all you care about!" exclaimed Mrs Bilge.

The stricken fisherman squeezed water from his beard and shivered as it dripped from his hand.

"I owe my crew the honour of telling the whole terrible tale."

Everybody fell silent and shuffled closer as if a performance was starting. The fisherman took a deep breath and began.

"We were fishing our usual route, sure enough, nets cast and filling steady with fat fish like jewelled fruit of the fertile sea. The sun was shining bright and true. All signs pointed to a day fine as a golden—"

Mrs Leech tapped her watch. "Perhaps we could hurry this along to the deadly attack?"

"We were getting ready to turn for home, when our nets snagged on something under the water," the fisherman continued. "Something big."

Alex held his breath, frightened of what the story might reveal.

"Oh, we tugged and we toiled to haul in our prize catch. To no avail! Until all at once it surfaced in a fuming torrent. The whole crew abandoned their post to stare in wonder. The Water Dragon rising beside our humble boat!"

The crowd waited in anxious silence as the fisherman paused to catch his breath. Anil continued to furiously take notes.

"What are you doing?" Zoey demanded.

"Writing down a new Haven Bay legend." The pen scratched. "Before the details get changed beyond recognition in retelling."

"Quiet!" Mrs Leech ordered, then nodded for the fisherman to continue.

"The dragon was long enough to tie a bow around the world! Its eyes blazed with fury and its teeth were sharp as broken glass."

Mrs Bilge gasped in dismay. "It ate our innocent fishermen!"

"The dragon would never—" Alex began to protest.

Mr Ballister shushed him so vehemently that his false teeth flew from his mouth and hit Alex in the chest. Kraken reared up and returned the favour with a sharp jet of water into the old man's empty mouth.

"Sinister clouds boiled up from nowhere to choke the sky," the fisherman intoned. "Wave and wind were whipped into a frenzy, tossing our humble craft like a cork."

The Water Dragon *could* summon a storm. The locals had seen it for themselves in the mouth of Haven Bay. But Alex knew that had only been to stop Callis from capturing it. The dragon wouldn't use it against innocent people for no reason.

"We begged the dragon to spare our wretched souls, but its storm only grew in vengeance. Our boat was flung away like a cannon shot." The fisherman whimpered. "I fell down into the hold and hit my head. By the time I made it back on deck the entire crew had disappeared! Then the luckless boat capsized and sent me into the water."

Anil scanned his notes. "Your crew disappeared *after* the boat was blown away from the dragon and *before* it capsized?"

The fisherman quivered. "Wherever they went, I didn't follow. Thank heavens the lifeboat crew claimed me before the ravenous clutches of the hungry deep."

"The deep isn't the only thing that's ravenously hungry," Bridget said, peeling open a protein bar.

"The dragon is a menace," said Mrs Bilge, wringing her hands before pointing at Alex. "How do we know you're not doing its bidding?"

"The Water Dragon doesn't want to hurt us. I think…"

The fisherman's story had confirmed his worst fear: the dragon was infected.

It would never break its connection with Alex unless something forced it. Even when the dragon was recovering from a grievous injury, Alex had been able to sense it out there. Now, the dragon was an *absence*.

If the parasites had taken the dragon over, surely they would take control of its magic too. It could be an unstoppable weapon in helping them spread all over the world.

Alex scanned the crowd. Maybe the time for secrets had passed. Trying to hide the truth would only allow fear to grow. He steeled himself before he spoke again.

"I think there's something wrong with the dragon. Something in the water that's making the sea animals behave strangely has infected it too."

"What if it attacks the town again like it did all those years ago?" said Mr Ballister.

Mrs Bilge dabbed a handkerchief against her cheek. "We can't let it take any more people."

Alex searched the crowd for any sympathetic faces. The argument was quickly slipping away from him. But he had to try one last time to convince them that the Water Dragon – that he and his sea magic – were no danger.

"We're going to find out why the dragon summoned that storm and where the fishermen have gone. We'll work out what's going on and we'll stop it," Alex said. "Then you'll see for yourselves that the Water Dragon – that *we* – are on your side."

Mrs Bilge sobbed. "Please find my grandson."

The crowd moved to comfort her. Bridget took the opportunity to scoop up the fisherman like a baby and lift him onto a trolley for Gene to push towards the medical room inside the harbour office. Then she turned to her brother.

"You should probably get out of here." She gripped his shoulders and steered him quickly out of the crowd, nodding for Zoey, Anil and Grandpa to follow.

"People will believe any old nonsense when they're scared," Grandpa said as they hurried away. "Sometimes the more yer try to convince 'em otherwise, the more yer push 'em to believe exactly what they want."

A moonless night had settled over the town. From the boatyard dock, the lights of the town curved away in a speckled arc. The lighthouse at the mouth of the bay swept the dark ocean in fleeting trails.

"If the dragon is already infected, we have to save it before it attacks any more boats," Alex said.

"Did it actually attack?" Anil studied his notes. "The fisherman said the storm pushed them away from the dragon. The capsizing might have been an accident. If the dragon really wanted to attack the boat, we all know it wouldn't have had any trouble destroying it."

"So maybe the dragon just didn't want the fishermen near it," Zoey said.

"Because if it's infected, it's safer to be as far away as possible."

Zoey punched Anil's shoulder. "Why didn't you say any of this back there, instead of making it a creative writing exercise?"

"As long as we don't know what's happened to the missing crew, the fisherman's story is going to spread." Anil tapped his notebook. "Stories like that are powerful. It's better that the story people remember – the one that becomes legend – is told by somebody who knows the truth."

Zoey thought about this for a moment. "Can I be a few inches taller in the story version? And maybe breathe fire?"

"I think most people who know you would believe it."

Alex grabbed Anil's notebook and reread the account. He had been so wrapped up in worrying that he hadn't listened properly to the details.

"Maybe the dragon isn't lost just yet," Alex said. "Before it broke our connection, I felt it fighting. If it's strong enough to push the fishermen away, it must be strong enough to try to hold off the parasites."

"For how long?" Zoey asked.

"Hopefully long enough for us to help. I know the dragon told me to stay away, but we have to go to it."

"First we need to work out where it is," Anil said.

"When Meri called, it sounded like she was near the baby dragon," said Zoey. "That means she can't have been far away from the Water Dragon. If we find *The Dragonfly*, we can find out everything Meri knows and then search."

"The lifeboat station can trace distress calls," Bridget said. "It takes a while, but I'll radio Gene to start as soon as they can."

"If yer can work out where Meri might be," said Grandpa, "I reckon I've got a way to get us there."

"And I'll go and speak to Argosy to see if he's found anything about a cure for the parasites," Anil said.

"We have to be ready to set off from the boatyard at first light," Alex said.

Once again, they had half a plan that he simply had to hope would work out.

"Time for adventure?" asked Zoey.

"Danger, daring and wet underpants," confirmed Alex. "The usual."

CHAPTER SIX

NO STRANGERS TO TROUBLE

Back at the boatyard, Loaf was missing.

"He must be here somewhere!" Zoey overturned pieces of junk as if the seal might be hiding underneath.

Bridget wrinkled her nose. "This is even more disgusting than I'd have guessed."

Zoey flushed bright red and hastily tried to wipe the grease off her hands, which only smeared it liberally across the front of her waders.

"We moved the seal to somewhere more comfortable." Mrs Wu stood in the doorway and beckoned for them to follow her. She led them through the back office and into a mechanic's garage. Shelves and racks of tools covered the walls. A deep, square pit set into the middle of the room would usually have been used for working underneath vehicles. Now it was filled halfway up with water. Old tyres had been piled up in one corner, providing a dry spot for Loaf to lounge, freed of his seaweed shackles.

"It's deep enough that he can't get out," said Mrs Wu. "I tried a few herbal remedies to soothe him. Bladderwrack paste, boiled ginger and brown sugar, the mint leaves your dad chews for his bad breath."

Loaf lifted his head and brayed indignantly. Alex caught an unmistakeable whiff of minty freshness. On his shoulder, Kraken flushed light green to match.

"Thank you for looking after him," he said.

Zoey squeezed her mum in a vice-like hug. "I know he'll be safe with you."

Beyond the garage, a row of rusted metal sheds lined the far side of the yard, pushed against the seafront. Alex had always assumed they sheltered boats awaiting repair or simply sat empty. So it was a surprise when Grandpa broke away without a word to cross towards them.

"Where are you going?" Alex and the others hurried after him.

Grandpa made for the last shed in the row and fished a chunky ring of keys from his pocket.

"I know it's 'ere somewhere," he said, sliding keys around the ring.

"What's here?" asked Alex.

"The key for this shed."

"No, I mean, what's here in the shed?"

"Yer'll find out when I find the right key."

Alex huffed impatiently and waited while Grandpa dismissed a succession of small silver keys, large brass keys and keys in strange shapes that didn't look like they would fit any lock in the world.

"Gotcha!" Grandpa crowed, lifting a key that looked to be made entirely of rust.

He spat onto the key, rubbed it vigorously on his sleeve (leaving behind a large, wet copper stain) and pushed it into the shed lock. It clunked open without any complaint. But when Grandpa pushed the door, it didn't budge.

"How about yer put those muscles to good use?"

Bridget eyed the rusty door with distaste and tugged her sleeves up over her hands. When she leaned her weight against it, the door scraped open, hinges screeching. It was more of a hatch, opening up inside a set of larger double doors.

"Mr Wu let me keep it 'ere," Grandpa said. "S'pose I probably owe him a couple of decades' rent."

They ducked through the hatch. Dust furred the air and made Alex cough. Light shafted across the inside of the shed from gaps in the metal roof.

A boat sat in the middle of the shed. The hull, twice as tall as Alex, was scabbed with peeling green paint, the wood underneath pitted with rot. Metal joints hung rusty and loose. Mouldy ropes and twisted chains trailed from the deck and a window was missing from the crooked cockpit.

"It smells like birds have nested in here," Alex said, wrinkling his nose.

"Or my dad's work boots," added Zoey.

"I've found out way too much about your dad's personal hygiene in the last five minutes," Bridget muttered.

If Grandpa heard them, he gave no sign. He began a long lap of the boat, running his fingers along its blemished hull.

"She might not look much." Grandpa turned to face them and swelled up with pride. "But she's how we're gonna hit the waves."

A pigeon, disturbed by the noise, flustered out of the cockpit and flapped away through the hatch.

"Does it...float?" asked Alex. That seemed like an important quality in any boat.

A rope ladder hung down the side of the boat from the deck above. Grandpa gripped it and clambered up with surprising agility, wiry arms pushing open a section of rusted rail so everybody else could climb aboard.

"She came 'ere as scrap, barely worth even that," said

Grandpa. "Instead of breakin' her down, I asked if I could build her back up."

The deck was dusty, littered with feathers and white spatters of bird mess. But the boards felt sturdy under Alex's feet. There *was* something promising about the boat, lying just underneath the surface. It made him think of himself – nobody would look at him and guess at the power he could wield.

"I thought one day yer grandma might want – might *need* – to get out on the sea again." Grandpa gazed dreamily around the deck. "I wanted to make sure she'd have a sound vessel to carry her safe. S'pose I have neglected her a bit since yer grandma..."

Alex took Grandpa's hand and squeezed it. "She's beautiful."

"She's exactly what we need!" said Zoey.

"She's totally gross," Bridget scoffed. Then she smiled. "But she's got character."

Grandpa wiped his eyes on the back of his hand. "With a little work, she'll take us in pursuit of the Water Dragon and whatever trouble we find there."

Alex and Zoey exchanged an uneasy look. Neither of them was a stranger to trouble and together they usually found a way to overcome it. But this time, the odds would be stacked against them worse than ever.

"The Water Dragon might not be on our side," Alex blurted. The thought had been nagging at him since trying to contact the dragon the night before. "It felt like it was barely resisting the parasites. If they completely take it over... We had a hard enough time stopping Loaf after he turned against us. The dragon could smash this boat to pieces without a second thought if it wanted."

"So we don't waste any time. We make this hunk of beautiful junk seaworthy by the time Gene traces *The Dragonfly*'s distress call and Anil has got any information about the cure from Argosy." Determination burned in Zoey's eyes. "Then we get out there while the dragon is still on our team."

Alex took a deep breath of musty air. The pressure of everything – the infected Water Dragon, the missing baby dragon, the worry for Meri – was almost too much. He dipped into the deep well of sea magic inside him, finding comfort in its strength.

"Let's get to work."

Alex, Zoey and Bridget followed Grandpa's instructions to clear the deck, board up the broken windows and scrape away rust and bird droppings. Mr Wu joined them to help repair the hull, patching up holes and replacing nails to make the vessel seaworthy again.

After a couple of hours, the double doors of the shed

banged open. The boatyard's lights poured inside, broken by the silhouettes of Anil, Erasmus Argosy and a forklift carrying an enormous crate.

"Cool!" Anil exclaimed, running to admire the boat.

Argosy looked considerably less enthusiastic. "This is our berth?"

"Nobody invited you to come," Grandpa growled.

The two older men shared a rancorous relationship. The close confines of the boat were unlikely to improve the situation.

Mr Wu expertly piloted the forklift to deposit the wooden crate carefully onto the deck. The entire boat seemed to sag under its weight.

"That better be snacks," Bridget said.

"The Argosy archive is too big to search through before we leave." Anil climbed up onto the deck and helped Erasmus to join him. "So we decided to bring the archive with us."

"*We* did not decide," Argosy grumbled. "Somehow, you convinced me."

He prised open the crate lid. Inside, books were stacked haphazardly, folders brimmed with papers and photographs and piles of newspaper teetered. Kraken immediately moved to jump inside and explore but Argosy barred her way.

"This material was collected by generations of my family. It is the most comprehensive history of sea magic in existence," Argosy lectured. "Under any other circumstances I would never remove it from the house. But I understand time is of the essence. As long as you all understand that the archive is delicate and must be protected at all costs."

"Boring." Bridget yawned.

Kraken waved an arm dismissively to suggest she agreed.

While the final repairs were made, Mrs Wu handed out packed lunches and stocked the pantry with tins of vegetables and bars of chocolate. Mr and Mrs Chatterjee delivered a comprehensive first aid kit.

"Are you sure it's safe?" asked Mrs Chatterjee, eyes scanning the numerous health and safety hazards of the dilapidated boat.

"Quite safe," Argosy called from on deck. Grandpa narrowed his eyes suspiciously, surprised to have the support of his nemesis. But Anil's parents accepted Argosy's word. Apparently they trusted the old man more than Alex did.

Lastly, Alex's dad brought some inflatable rings, life jackets and a large fish tank they could fill with safe water for Kraken. The otters arrived with him, immediately scampering up to explore the boat.

"I'm really not sure about this," said Alex's dad. "You don't even know how long you'll be gone."

The other parents overheard and Alex saw the same doubt creeping into their expressions.

"We're going to be well supervised by two responsible adults!" Alex said quickly.

"Who?" asked Grandpa, fishing inside his ear for a glob of wax. "Oh, me."

"They'll be perfectly safe with us!" Argosy waved from the deck, almost overbalancing and just catching himself before he fell over the rail.

Amazingly, Alex's dad still didn't look convinced.

"You've seen what's happened around here over the last few months," said Alex. "This is bigger than any of it. If we don't save the Water Dragon..."

Sooner or later, the dragon would no longer be able to resist the parasites. It would fall under their control and its immense power would be a danger to the entire world.

"I don't *want* to sail off into terrible danger. But there's nobody else that can do it," Alex concluded. "I'm the only one with sea magic. And we're the only people who care enough about the dragon to try and save it."

Alex's dad still didn't look happy, but he nodded all the same. "What should we tell your school?"

A strong hand with immaculately painted nails slapped

onto his shoulder. "Tell them everybody has explosive diarrhoea."

Bridget grinned and sauntered past. She had changed into a blue and white stripey jumper, cut-off shorts covered in embroidered anchors and a sailor's cap tilted jauntily to one side over hair tied into an elaborate braid.

"I didn't even see you leave," Alex said.

"I thought I'd better look the part for our epic voyage." Bridget waved over her shoulder. "Plus I thought we should bring somebody with actual sailing expertise."

Gene Lennox shuffled into the shed, swaddled in a heavy anorak, flip-flops slapping on the concrete floor. Chonkers, the Neptune family cat, clung to their face with her claws.

"A ship's cat is good luck," said Gene, spitting out a mouthful of fur. They held up a sheet of paper. "I found *The Dragonfly*'s location from when it sent the distress call."

Zoey snatched and read the page. "They're maybe a day's sailing away if they haven't gone too far."

It took another hour to hastily patch the hull and repair the engine. When everything was securely loaded, the archive crate strapped down under a tent-like plastic sheet to keep it from getting wet and the fish tank set up to Kraken's liking, Mr Wu led them in pushing a metal frame full of rollers underneath the boat. Once in place, the boat rolled forward along two rails towards the front of the shed, where a stopping block held it in place.

Next, the front doors were opened wide, revealing the placid water of the bay waiting to receive them. The sky was turning pink with first light on the horizon.

Everybody assembled on the shed floor in the shadow of the boat.

Mr Wu asked them to wait as he hurried off towards his office, returning a moment later with a pot of paint and a brush. He handed them to Grandpa.

"We noticed the boat's name has faded."

The hull had been hastily patched without any time to repaint it. On the side of the bow, a metal plate was screwed crookedly in place. Faint, looping letters hinted at the name once written there.

Grandpa plucked out the brush and repainted the letters in a single, practised motion.

Dorothea.

The name of Alex's grandma.

Alex and his dad pulled Grandpa into a hug, Bridget wrapping them all up in her mighty arms. The others hugged their respective parents goodbye.

Finally, the voyaging party gathered on deck in preparation to leave.

Alex spotted something large to one side of the deck,

hidden underneath a dusty sheet. When he tried to peek under it, Grandpa slapped his hands away.

"It's nothin' interestin'. Just make sure you keep away from it on pain of death."

Alex ducked around him and whipped the sheet away. Underneath was one of the old ship's cannons that usually decorated the top of the Haven Bay sea wall. The weapons had been stolen and reactivated by the pirates before being returned following Callis's defeat.

"En't a proper ship without a cannon," Grandpa said sheepishly. "Nobody noticed one still missin'."

"Lots of people noticed," Alex corrected him. "They've been looking for it for a month."

Zoey bounded across the deck to stroke the cannon as if it was an enormous dog. "Bagsy I get to fire it!"

Outside, the sun peeked above the horizon to shine across the bay. The water didn't reflect it back, as if the tainted sea had trapped it beneath the surface.

Mr Wu positioned himself by the stopping block. "Ready?"

The entire crew turned to Alex for the final word.

He nodded. "Ready."

"Hang on a minute," Anil said. "Did anybody check that the boat is actually seaworthy?"

Too late. The block was kicked away and the boat

leaned onto the rollers. She slid along the rails, slowly at first, before tilting sharply down and rushing towards the waiting waves. Spray stung their faces as she splashed into the bay.

Everybody held their breath.

The boat rocked side to side, as if finding her sea legs, before she settled level and bobbed soundly on the swell.

"That's my girl!" whooped Grandpa.

A cheer went up, both on deck and behind them in the shed, as the boat's engine grumbled, coughed and then growled to life to whisk them towards the mouth of the bay, in search of *The Dragonfly* and a pair of dragons.

CHAPTER SEVEN

MOTLEY CREW

The inevitable argument began as the ocean swell grew higher beyond the lighthouse, the boat rising and falling in affable harmony with the waves.

"I should obviously be captain!" insisted Zoey.

Bridget scoffed. "Give me exactly seventy-three reasons why."

"I'm a mechanical genius, my authority is feared and respected by all, I look dashing in a variety of hats—" Zoey counted the reasons off on her fingers.

"Don't *actually* give me seventy-three!"

Gene cleared their throat, keeping both hands firmly on the boat's wheel. "May I point out that, so far, I'm the only one who's done any actual sailing?"

"No, you may not," Bridget replied, adjusting her sailor's hat. "A captain should be strong and beautiful as well as, like, good at boats or whatever."

"You're only good at *crashing* boats," Gene pointed out.

Bridget smiled at them fondly. "Two out of three isn't bad."

Alex was happy to stay out of the running. There would be enough for him to deal with today without trying to turn them all into a competent crew. Instead, he leaned against the rail and watched Haven Bay grow smaller behind them. The familiar arc of the bay rapidly flattened to a hazy smudge of land on the horizon.

Before the awakening of his magic, Alex had been too frightened to dip a toe into the sea. It was still exciting – *liberating* – to set out upon the open ocean. This was where he truly belonged.

But it was bittersweet to watch Haven Bay fade from view. Increasingly, it seemed his powers made him an outsider there. What if nobody welcomed him home when he eventually returned?

Zoey's voice woke him from his reverie. "Meri is in danger! I should be in charge!"

The argument was loud enough to bring Grandpa up from below decks. After a few moments of looking between Alex at the rail and the captaincy debate, he lifted crooked fingers to his lips and blew a sharp whistle to snatch everybody's attention.

"*I'm* the captain of this ship!" Grandpa told them, firmly enough that nobody would argue. "Apparently I'm the only responsible adult on board."

"Excuse me," Argosy called from the bow.

"I'll *excuse you* to walk the plank if yer challenge my authority. Now, we've got a long way to sail and I won't have yer frettin' and feudin' the whole way. It's time to assign jobs to keep yer busy."

Grandpa cracked his knuckles – *crunch pop pop!* – and pointed to Gene.

"We don't wanna sink, so you're in charge of steerin'." Then he pointed between them each in turn. "Bridget, there's some heavy stuff in the hold what needs movin' around. Zoey, I've got some stuff for yer to fix. Anil—"

"I want him with me," Argosy called.

Anil had already been lingering near the square tent of plastic sheeting at the front of the boat that sheltered the archive crate. Now he beamed with delight.

"The archive is in disarray," Argosy continued. "Young Mr Chatterjee has shown a remarkable ability to piece together even the most disparate scraps of information. If the cure for the parasites resides within these records, he is the one who will find it."

68

"All right, take him," Grandpa growled.

Anil punched the air and immediately ran to retrieve a leather-bound tome from the crate.

"What should I do?" asked Alex.

Grandpa held up a mop and a packet of yellow rubber gloves. "This boat could use a spring clean."

Alex had hoped his magical powers might qualify him for a more exciting task, but he was still willing to do his bit. Anything was better than standing around and worrying.

"How about a sea shanty to get us motivated?" offered Grandpa.

"Please, no," Bridget said.

Grandpa began stamping his foot to create a rhythmic *thump-thump-thump* before he broke into song.

"Come all ye young people who follow the sea,
Wey hey, from danger we never run!
And pray pay attention I'm sure you'll agree,
We'll save our precious dragon!"

Grandpa's voice sounded like an anchor being dragged across an iceberg. He waved for everybody else to join in the song.

"We don't know the words." Zoey winced.

"Even if I did, I wouldn't embarrass myself by singing them," added Bridget.

Before starting the second verse, Grandpa scooped up Chonkers, her warbling protest accompanying his stamping foot.

"We've sailors and otters and seagulls and all,
Ready to fight for our mates!
We'll best any enemy, obstacle or squall,
Yo ho! We sail to our fates!"

Before Grandpa could launch into another verse, his stamping foot broke through the deck and lodged in the wood. Chonkers yowled and wriggled from his grip.

"Uh, somethin' else for yer to fix."

Zoey sighed and moved to help dislodge him. Everybody else went off to their assigned posts, leaving Alex to snap on a pair of rubber gloves, drop to his knees and scrub the grimy deck. It was caked with dirt, and he scoured the boards until his arms ached, water sluicing away black. At least it kept his eyes from the lapping ocean, and he tried not to notice that land was no longer in sight. It was easier to scrub than to worry about what they might find over the horizon.

The animals refused to be left out. Kraken waved to be removed from her tank so she could spray a steady fountain of water from his shoulder, while the otters slid back and forth in the soapy froth, using their bodies as brushes. Chonkers climbed to the cockpit roof to serve as lookout.

After an hour or so, Alex's methodical scrubbing brought him close to the archive tent. Kraken hopped back into her tank stationed beside the crate. Anil sat cross-legged on a plastic groundsheet, surrounded by newspapers and books, a sheaf of papers in his lap.

"I'm surprised you weren't competing for the captaincy too," Alex said.

"It was tempting! I've even got a bird companion." Pinch landed on Anil's shoulder and pooped a white streak down his back. "But I think I'm best at doing this."

"At reading?"

"Records and stories and legends are how we understand the world." Anil swept his gaze over the books scattered around him. "Piecing together a complete history of the town, as well as everything known about sea magic, will do more than just guide us. It can stop everybody making the same mistakes they've been repeating for decades."

Alex brushed his fingers against the rough wood of the archive crate. "Do you really think the answer to saving the world is in there?"

"I know I'm going to find it." Anil thumped the book closed. "Somehow, this all just makes sense to me. One record gives me a hint and suddenly I *know* where to find the map or diary entry that confirms it. You've got your awesome powers and Zoey's got her amazing inventions. I think this is how *I* can really make a difference."

Alex smiled. This wasn't like Anil's usual boasting. This was genuine pride and belief.

"Then read as fast as you can," Alex said. "When you write our story, just try and make it sound like I knew what I was doing."

Anil grinned. "Deal. I've actually been thinking about writing a play to show everybody all the amazing stuff you've done. Remember when you raised an army of water troops to help break the dragon out of the aquarium, then tied up Callis's goons with seaweed? Nobody could be scared of you if they knew about that!"

"I think that story might *make* people scared of me," said Alex.

"They'll be much more frightened of the Water Dragon if we don't find a way to cure it." Argosy's voice came from inside the crate. "It will be a danger to the entire world."

Alex felt his hackles rise. "You make it sound like the dragon is our enemy."

Argosy's eyes peeked over the lip of the crate. "We might have no choice but to consider it so."

There wasn't time to argue before a *thump* inside the

72

crate made Argosy yelp and drop out of sight. Papers rustled and tumbled.

"I think I might be stuck," he called.

"Leave him in there." Grandpa strode along the deck, arms behind his back, Bridget and Gene in tow. Bridget had slung a burly arm casually around Gene's shoulders and they talked with their heads pushed close together. Zoey trailed behind, glowering at their backs.

"Yer've earned a break," Grandpa announced. When he revealed his hands, they held ice cream cones instead of cleaning implements.

"You installed the ice cream machine on the boat?" said Alex.

"I was gonna bring the chimes too but there wasn't time."

They stood together at the rail, licking their ice creams in appreciative silence. Chonkers, who had come to lap up any drips, yawned extravagantly and triggered everybody to do the same. Nobody had slept for well over twenty-four hours. At least the sugar would perk them up.

The ocean stretched in every direction, shimmering faintly under a hazy sun. It managed to be both impossibly vast and reassuringly intimate, lapping softly against the gently swaying hull.

"The Water Dragon told me to stay away," Alex said.

Zoey wiped ice cream from her lips. "I sense the approach of a classic Alex Neptune self-doubt moment that we have to talk you out of."

"It's not my fault you've never experienced self-doubt in your entire life."

She shrugged. "It's true."

"This time I'm sure we're doing the right thing. We have to try and help the dragon. But..."

"We can't give you a pep talk if you trail off mysteriously," Bridget admonished.

"The infected animals become aggressive. Even Loaf tried to fight us off." They had left the seal under the care of Zoey's parents so at least he was safe. "What if the dragon can't keep resisting the parasites and turns against us too? Against *me*? I'm getting stronger – I believe in my power – but it will never be enough to take down the dragon if we have to."

Zoey thought for a moment. "The dragon will do everything it can to avoid hurting us, even if something else is trying to force it. And, if it comes to it, I think you're way stronger than you realize."

"Not as strong as me," Bridget muttered beside them.

"Whatever happens," Zoey continued, "we'll do what we always do."

"Fumble along and hope everything somehow works out against impossible odds?"

74

"Well, sort of. We'll do everything we can to find a way to *win*. Even if it's scary or hopeless or weird."

"How long until we reach *The Dragonfly*'s last location?" asked Alex.

"We've made good time." Zoey checked her watch. "If nothing bad happens, we should get there before nightfall."

Beside her, Anil groaned loudly.

"Brain freeze?" she asked.

"No! Well, yes, a bit." He had already finished his ice cream and Pinch was busy eating the cone. "You should know better than to say *if nothing bad happens*. Now something bad is definitely going to happen!"

"Not necessarily." Zoey huffed. "You're so obsessed with things going wrong that you can't even imagine that maybe everything...will...be..."

She trailed off. Everybody stared wordlessly at Anil. As Zoey had been talking, his hair had begun to lift from his scalp in perfectly straight, upright strands. Now it formed a halo around his head.

"Is there ice cream on my face?" he asked, wiping at his cheeks.

Slowly, everybody's hair lifted as if being pulled by ghosts. Kraken's skin turned a shocking yellow and the otters puffed up into bristly round balls. Alex felt his skin tingle, static itching at his fingertips.

"It took me ages to style my hair!" Bridget complained, squashing it down onto her scalp.

Her elbow brushed the metal rail and she yelped as a spark of electricity crackled against her skin.

"Everybody away from the rail," Alex said.

Keeping his hands away, he peered over the side.

A long, tube-like fish followed the boat, its thick body snaking through the water to keep pace. Frilly fins billowed down the length of its belly. A snub-nosed face with a deep, powerful jaw lifted from the water to meet his gaze.

"It's an eel," Alex said.

A small, blue lightning bolt fizzed from the eel's body. The charge snapped up the metal joints of the boat's hull and hummed across the wet deck.

"An *electric* eel," Zoey said, appearing beside him. "Cool."

Anil stepped up on Alex's other side. "You see, straight away, something bad happens."

"If you're saying I can prophesy eels then I take it as a compliment."

"It's only one," Alex said. He had researched electric eels back when the ocean was his enemy. "By itself, it's not powerful enough to hurt us."

"Speak for yourself," Bridget grumbled, rubbing her elbow.

The water around the boat writhed and bubbled. What

Alex had thought were grey waves revealed themselves to be more quick-swimming bodies. Eels surrounded them on all sides and easily matched their pace.

"And how powerful are a whole army of them?" asked Zoey.

Before Alex could answer, electricity crackled from the eel armada and surged towards the boat.

CHAPTER EIGHT

A SHOCKING ENCOUNTER

Zoey grabbed both Alex and Anil to propel them tumbling onto the groundsheet of the plastic tent.

"Get off the deck!" she bellowed.

Bridget scooped up Grandpa and Gene (one under each arm) before jumping underneath the tent. The otters followed, grabbing Chonkers on the way. Kraken was already secure inside her tank.

Electricity crackled across the deck in pursuit, wet boards sizzling and pouring steam. It fizzed in snapping webs between rails and cables, sparked from nails and buzzed on the air like a swarm of sandflies.

"Is everybody okay?" asked Alex.

They had collided into a heap on the plastic groundsheet.

The thin covering was enough to insulate them from the electricity enveloping the rest of the deck.

Bridget pulled Zoey upright. "That was quick thinking."

"When you've electrocuted yourself as many times as I have, eventually you learn to avoid it."

"I feel like I just always knew not to electrocute myself," Anil said.

Carefully, everybody stood up and huddled together on their insulated island, elbows bumping and feet shuffling to keep away from the edge of the sheet. The eels swarmed the sides of the boat, tumbling over each other as they fired their deadly charge.

"Why are they doing this?" asked Gene.

"They must be infected. There's no other reason to attack us," said Alex. "We have to get to the controls and get away from them."

The throb of the engine beneath their feet sputtered. The boat jolted as it tried to maintain power, before the noise fell away altogether, leaving nothing but the fierce hum of electricity. Slowly, they drifted to a halt. The eels crowded close.

"Oh, heck," said Zoey. "I think the excess electricity has stalled the engine."

"Everybody *stop* saying your immediate plans out loud," Anil implored. "It only makes them go instantly wrong."

Zoey looked to Alex. "Can you use your powers to get us away?"

"I'd have to touch the water." He could summon a wave to scatter the eels or carry the boat to safety. But if he tried now, he'd get electrocuted. "We need to get the engine working again."

The cockpit was only a short distance away, but the entire deck crawled with electricity. A smell like burnt toast was beginning to fill the air.

"If you can get me there, I can probably fix it," said Zoey. She took a pair of rubber gloves from the packet and shoved them into her pocket.

"I could throw you," Bridget suggested. "You're only little."

"I'm not *that* little!"

Alex cast around for inspiration. The safe zone contained nothing but the plastic sheeting, the crate of archive material and...

A tank of seawater.

"You know that cage you built in your workshop?" Alex asked Zoey. "Did it really stop you getting electrocuted?"

"Ninety-three per cent of the time, yes. It's a mesh of conductive material that distributes the charge so anything inside doesn't get shocked."

"And water conducts electricity, right?"

Zoey glanced at the eels pushing against the side of the boat. "Obviously."

Alex scooped Kraken out of the tank and handed her to Grandpa. "I need to use your water," he told her. "I'll make it up to you afterwards."

The octopus curled an arm in what might have been a thumbs up.

Alex thrust a hand into the tank. A small flare of sea magic made the water cling to his hand like a glove. Carefully, he lifted it from the tank and used his other hand to stretch the water into a long, thick bar. Then he flexed his fingers and a thread of water spiralled loose from the bar like a shoot growing from soil.

Sweat beaded on Alex's forehead. Never before had he attempted such fine control of his magic. He held his focus to tease out more threads to run alongside the first like bars in a cage.

"Zoey," he said through gritted teeth.

His best friend understood and stepped up close beside him.

The bars of water closed around them, looping over their heads and dropping to the ground, until they were both encased inside a perpetually flowing cage.

"Is this going to work?" Alex asked.

"We're in for a shock if it doesn't," Zoey replied.

Together, they stepped off the plastic sheet. Although he was no longer touching the water, Alex held its new shape in his mind. The cage moved with them. Its bars touched the bare deck to redirect the electricity there. It surged up and over their heads, close enough that Alex felt his eyebrows stand on end, before arcing around to flow back into the wet deck. A complete circuit that meant the current bypassed them completely.

"Everybody stay here," Alex instructed.

"We don't exactly have a choice," muttered Grandpa.

"What's happening out there?" called Argosy from where he was still stuck inside the crate. "It sounds bad."

Grandpa sighed. "I s'pose I better rescue him."

The water cage was small enough that Alex and Zoey were pressed together, forcing them to shuffle awkwardly along the deck, keeping a steady pace to ensure neither of them accidentally broke the protective circuit. Over the rail, the eels seemed to sense them stepping out into the open, the crackle of their electricity intensifying.

Inside the cockpit, the wheel drifted listlessly. A narrow set of steps in the floor led down to the engine. Alex and Zoey shimmied around into single file within the cage. Zoey went first, forcing Alex to duck as the cage dipped low and sizzled on his hair.

"No smoke," Zoey said, studying the engine. "That's usually a good sign."

Electricity rolled across the wires and casing of the engine. Alex gently flexed a bar of their cage to touch the metal and divert the flow away. Zoey snapped on her rubber gloves to be sure.

"I'll try a manual restart," she said, fiddling with a wire. She flicked a switch and then pressed a green button as hard as she could. The engine grumbled, belched, but didn't start. Zoey adjusted a few more wires and tried again. No luck.

"It needs a jump start," she said.

"Hang on. The problem is a *lack* of electricity?"

"Not exactly. There's too much of it going everywhere rather than where it needs to be. We have to focus the whole lot into the battery."

Alex sighed. "I've got a really stupid idea."

"A stupid idea that might actually work?"

"Just keep those gloves on and follow me."

Back at the top of the steps, Alex leaned out of the cockpit door. The eels showed no sign of tiring. Electricity still strafed the deck. In places, the wood appeared to have dried out, charred black lines smouldering through the boards. If they waited much longer it might catch fire.

"Everybody put on some rubber gloves!" Alex shouted.

Grandpa grabbed the packet and handed out gloves. Anil and Bridget shoved some spares onto the otter's heads like frilled hats.

"Now I need somebody to grab an eel."

Everybody blinked at him incredulously.

"From down there?" asked Anil.

"Not quite," Alex said.

A throaty *whoomph* made them all jump. Fire sprang up in the middle of the deck, chewing through dry patches of the boards.

"Keep it away from the archive!" Argosy squeaked.

"We'll lose the whole boat if it spreads!" Grandpa roared.

But the electricity stopped them from tackling the blaze. The flames creeped towards the tent, heat billowing on the air.

"Be ready to catch!" Alex shouted.

He squatted down so he could reach the deck without breaking the water cage. There would be no time now for fine control. He needed to touch the damp boards as briefly as possible.

"How much is this going to hurt?" he asked.

Zoey winced. "It's probably best not to know."

Alex accepted that with a nod and then touched his fingers to the electrified deck. He released a current of sea magic at the same time as electricity leaped up his arm.

84

Clawing heat seared beneath his skin and he was flung backwards out of the cage.

"Alex!"

The magic surged overboard to reach the ocean and detonated underneath the waves. Water exploded upwards, throwing the eels into the air. The flow of electricity was broken at the same time as Alex landed hard against the boat's rail.

"Heads up!" shouted Zoey.

A wriggling, writhing rain of eels fell from the sky. Most had been blasted away from the boat, but a few were tumbling within reach.

Zoey lunged for one over the railing but it slipped through her grasp. Bridget hefted Gene onto her shoulders to try and pluck one from the air, but they couldn't quite reach.

A single eel fell towards the front of the boat, coming down just inside the rail. Right above Anil's head.

"Catch it!" Zoey shouted.

Anil cupped his hands in preparation. At the same moment, the fire blew towards the archive, flames catching some of the books and papers left out on the groundsheet.

"No!" Anil shouted, abandoning the catch to stamp at the blaze.

The eel bounced off his shoulder and looked as if it would flounder away over the side.

Quickly, the otters scrambled to form a chain, clinging to each other's tails. They leaped out over the rail far enough for the last otter to get his rubber-clad head underneath the eel and nudge it back towards deck.

Grandpa snatched it up. The eel wriggled in his grasp, sparking furiously, but its electricity couldn't penetrate the rubber gloves. Bridget grabbed it and prepared to throw.

"You better catch this!" she shouted to Zoey.

Bridget launched the eel with a rugby pass. Alex watched the eel spiral through the air, tiny forks of lightning crackling from its body, before Zoey caught it safely in both gloved hands.

She spun around, thumped down the cockpit steps, and pressed the eel directly to the engine.

The boat roared to life, its engine thrumming powerfully through the deck like it might shake itself loose.

Grandpa hurried to help Alex groggily to his feet, while Gene rushed past them to ready the boat for escape. Everybody else set about smothering the fire, as blackened pieces of the precious archive drifted into the air.

CHAPTER NINE

AN EXCELLENT PASTIE RECIPE

Once the fire was out and they were well clear of the eels, Gene brought the boat to a halt so they could assess the damage.

Blackened splits of burned wood braided the deck, a charred map of where the current had been strongest. Thankfully, the fire had not spread far; a smouldering hole in the deck could be easily patched and the plastic tent was only a little melted. A handful of books and papers had burned and Anil was busy salvaging what he could while Zoey and Gene checked over the engine.

"We should probably swap out the spark plugs," suggested Gene.

Zoey nodded appraisingly. "I suggest a full inspection of

the rear gasket cylinder head and a complete audit of driver housing clamp screws."

She peeked over a shoulder to check if Bridget was listening. The other girl was too busy scrubbing her chipped fingernails with a coarse brush.

"I think there's eel gunk in my cuticles," she whined.

"You were wearin' gloves," Grandpa pointed out.

"Out, gross spot! Out, I say!"

Alex had been excused from the clean-up on account of being slightly electrocuted. Every centimetre of his skin still tingled from the shock and his fingertips were numb. If he stood up, he wasn't sure his legs would hold him.

Grandpa slathered cold, sticky burn salve onto Alex's hand.

"Is this enough?" he called to Anil, undoubtedly the member of the crew with the most medical knowledge.

"More," Anil called back absent-mindedly, studying a singed leaf of paper.

Grandpa squeezed the tube as hard as he could, splattering salve all the way up to Alex's elbow.

"That seems like too much," Alex protested.

"Doctor's son's orders."

Next, Grandpa wound a long length of bandage around the wounded hand, swaddling it tight, salve squeezing out between the gaps. Kraken pawed at Alex's hand tenderly and pressed close to his cheek as if she would never leave him again.

"How many times a day do we need to change this bandage?" Grandpa called.

"Hmm?" Anil wiped soot from the cover of a book. "Oh, twenty?"

Grandpa frowned. "That seems a lot."

Night fell rapidly at sea, the horizon seeming to close around the boat each time Alex glanced away. Usually there would be other lights on the water, distant ships and lonely outposts. Tonight he saw none. The darkness promised to be absolute, as if they alone dared sail through the night. Maybe the recent storms and rumours of a vengeful dragon had kept everybody else on dry land.

Alex searched behind the boat, wondering if he might still be able to catch a glimpse of Haven Bay as its lights came on. But they had travelled too far from home.

"So do you have electrical powers now too?" Zoey asked, once the engine had been serviced and they were back on the move. She hovered a hand close to his skin as if expecting a shock.

"No, I just have pins and needles in my knees."

Zoey sat beside him on the deck, back pressed against the upright of the rail. "I've been thinking."

"Uh oh."

She lightly punched his arm, snatching her hand away at the snap of a static spark. "The infected animals back home could be aggressive, but it was usually only if they were provoked or people got too close. They never attacked for no reason, and never as a group like those eels."

"We must be getting closer to the dragon." Alex straightened a little. "They were trying to stop us before we could interfere. But how can they plan an attack like that?"

"There'd have to be a way for the parasites to communicate with each other between hosts."

Alex remembered how his connection to the infected animals – to the dragon – had felt blocked. There had been a presence there that he hadn't been able to identify. Now he wondered...

"Do we still have that eel?"

After using it to jump-start the engine, the eel had been dropped into Kraken's tank so that Zoey could study it. Alex, still slightly unsteady on his feet, approached it. On his shoulder, Kraken crossed her arms sulkily at having lost her tank.

Drops of water had run down the outside of the glass. Alex reached for them with his unbandaged hand. The eel crackled with electricity but the charge stayed safely contained within the tank.

The moment Alex touched the water, he felt the stifled

thread between him and the creature. He closed his eyes and pressed at the blockage with his magic, testing it for any sign of weakness. It held fast, his power waning when it came into contact.

But this time Alex was aware of another presence moving along the thread, like a louder voice shouting down the line so he or the dragon couldn't be heard.

"The parasites aren't just blocking the ocean threads." Alex opened his eyes. "They're using them to communicate between infected hosts."

"Which means you can't use them at all!" Zoey shook her head. "That's...really annoying."

Alex crouched to bring his gaze level with the eel. Its thick, flexible body shimmied from side to side to hold it in place.

"We're going to beat you," he told the parasites watching from behind the eel's eyes. "The dragon is still fighting you, so we'll fight with everything we have too."

"Because when the situation looks impossible, that's when you have to fight your hardest," Zoey said.

Together, with Kraken cheering them on, they tipped the electric eel overboard. It wriggled away as soon as it hit the water.

Alex looked around the boat. Lamps had been lit to wash the deck in orange light. At the helm, Bridget and

Gene talked in hushed voices, while Grandpa fussed over the cannon with an oily rag. The otters had teamed up with Chonkers to steal food from a cooler.

Beside the tank, Anil seemed to have finished gathering up the damaged records and was trying to lay them out in order.

"Did you lose anything important?" Alex asked.

"The problem is that we don't know exactly what *is* important." Anil sighed. "Even a couple of burned-up lines could be the difference between finding the cure tonight or in a week."

Alex was surprised to feel a flash of annoyance. Obviously the archive was important, but during the eel attack Anil's decision to protect it had almost lost their only chance of escape. It made Alex worry how much influence Erasmus Argosy might be developing over his friend.

Behind the crate, Argosy sat on a camping chair. There was a book open in his lap, but Alex was sure the old man was listening to their conversation.

A flap of wings brushed the tent roof as Pinch descended from the dark sky. The seagull held a lightly scorched fragment of paper in its beak.

"Great, you've brought me more litter." Anil took the paper, ready to scrunch it into a ball. Then he spotted something on the page and his eyes widened. "That's how I can find the right year."

"What do you mean?" Alex asked.

Anil grabbed a book and riffled through its pages, before jabbing his finger at a long list of barely legible handwriting.

"There was an assistant naturalist who kept a journal during an expedition around the Outer Hebrides. He refers to an article in the winter edition of the *Cornish Coastal Review* next to an excellent pastie recipe." Anil jumped up onto a stool to reach inside the crate, snatching up a stack of dog-eared magazines. "I know I've seen that somewhere."

"The pastie recipe?" asked Zoey, licking her lips.

"No, the article!"

Argosy got to his feet and came to watch Anil flip through the journals, dismissing each one in seconds when he didn't find what he needed. Alex wondered if they should help, but it seemed like they would only get in his way.

"Here!" Anil crowed, pointing triumphantly to a page dedicated mostly to hand-drawn depictions of sea snails. "And this article refers to a biologist who specialized in marine insects. But there's no name! If I had that, I could dig out their work and see if they knew about the parasites. Maybe if I find passenger lists for ferries in that area..."

Alex had seen Anil attempt to master countless hobbies over the last few months, but he had never seen him like this.

"It's like watching a composer put together a symphony," he said.

Zoey nodded. "Or a conspiracy theorist posting on an internet forum."

"I'm on the trail of the cure. This was the breakthrough I needed!" Anil hugged Pinch, squashing the seagull against his chest. "If there are no more distractions, I should be able to—"

Grandpa's voice rang along the deck from the stern of the boat. "Flotsam in the water! You better come and look at this!"

Anil sighed. "I knew I shouldn't have said it out loud."

They hurried to reach Grandpa at the back of the boat. Night had settled heavily on the water. Beyond the rail was total darkness, any trace of the world erased. Grandpa peered through an eyeglass into the inky black. Everybody peeled their eyes in the same direction.

"You can't possibly see anything," said Argosy.

"I ruddy well can!" Grandpa pointed. "Look."

Alex strained his eyes. There was nothing there. The absolute night almost made it impossible to imagine anything *could* be there.

Until he saw it. Faint and blinking in the distance.

A light bobbing on the water.

CHAPTER TEN

HI, *DRAGONFLY*

Alex grabbed the eyeglass and pressed it to his eye. It took a moment of scanning the dark waves before he found the light again. Pale green, it smouldered like fire inside a glass bottle drifting on the surf.

"It's seafire," he said.

Zoey leaned over the rail beside him. "We're close to *The Dragonfly*'s last location. Meri must have left seafire as a marker! Are there any more?"

Slowly, Alex swept the eyeglass across the magnified darkness behind the seafire. The waves were choppy enough that white foam kept snatching his attention, before it sizzled away to nothing. No further green lights materialized in the dark.

"Whenever we announce a plan, something goes wrong," Anil said behind him. "So maybe we should act like our plan is the opposite of what we really want to do."

"I don't think reverse psychology works on fate," said Zoey.

"All I know is that I *really* hope we *can't* find a trail of lights that leads us *right* to *The Dragonfly*." Anil lifted his voice as if wanting an eavesdropper to overhear. "There's no *way* our good friend Meri would be smart enough to do that."

Zoey huffed. "This is the most ridiculous—"

"Wait," Alex said.

A glimmer caught his attention. It flickered in and out of sight like a distant star, making it hard to focus the eyeglass. But Alex was sure he recognized it. Seafire!

"There's a trail!" he called, pointing into the night. "That way!"

Anil smiled smugly. "Fate fell for the oldest trick in the book."

"I absolutely *don't* want Bridget to realize how smart and cool I am," Zoey muttered under her breath, before glancing at the older girl hopefully.

The engine rumbled as Gene steered the boat to pursue the lights. Alex kept the eyeglass up. As the second light grew closer, he spotted a third green glow a short distance away.

"There!"

"What if we're too late?" Zoey spoke quietly enough that only Alex would hear. "It's been a long time since she called for our help."

Alex lowered the eyeglass. "We came as quickly as we could. Meri is brave and clever. She'll have found a way to keep her crew safe."

Alex raised the eyeglass again. The next seafire beacon seemed to bob more slowly, higher in the darkness than the others, almost as if it was hovering on the air.

Gradually, other shapes materialized around it: a dangling length of rope, a flat surface like a table, a round post that might have been the base of a mast. The seafire was on the deck of a ship.

"Ship ahoy." Alex was so relieved that his voice caught in his throat.

"Ship ahoy!" Grandpa bellowed, making his ears ring.

Zoey leaned so far over the railing it looked like she would fall overboard. "Is it *The Dragonfly*?"

"I can't tell."

Bridget snatched the eyeglass and squinted through it. "There's nobody on deck."

"It could be a trap." Anil stroked Pinch nervously, the seagull snoozing soundly on his shoulder. "We should wait until morning."

"There's no time." Zoey looked at the dozing seagull and smiled. "I've got an idea."

After hurrying to retrieve her bag, Zoey produced a small, round camera fixed to a headband. She looped it twice around Pinch's neck so that the camera sat on the gull's chest like a diamond necklace. A button press turned on a bright LED light that startled the bird awake.

"Get him to fly over the ship," instructed Zoey. "We can watch the camera feed on my laptop."

Anil (politely) gave the order. Pinch squawked grumpily but stretched his wings to lift lazily into the sky. The light around his neck pierced the darkness like a search plane as he closed the distance between vessels.

Zoey opened her laptop. The camera feed was dark and grainy, details fuzzing across the screen as light touched them: a deck cobbled together from mismatched pieces of wood; a bank of solar panels; a broken lamp post redeployed as a mast, holding sails knitted together from a patchwork of different materials.

"It's *The Dragonfly*!" Zoey cheered.

Alex kept his eyes on the screen. "But where's the crew?"

Nobody appeared on the video feed. Empty deck, empty rigging, empty crow's nest. The ship appeared completely abandoned.

"I bet it's haunted," said Bridget.

"A ship doesn't get haunted just 'cause it's been empty for a couple of days," Grandpa retorted.

"It does if the whole crew was eaten by sharks or selkies or—"

Alex nudged her to be quiet, nodding at Zoey, who had turned ghostly pale herself. They were already worried enough about Meri without Bridget making it worse.

Pinch returned to slam down on Anil's shoulder. Something long, dappled red and white, was clutched in his beak.

Bridget recoiled. "Is that a finger?"

"A crab claw." Anil took it from the seagull. The claw had been broken off at the base, the pincer half open.

"Do crabs eat people?" Bridget whispered.

"We can't waste any more time," Zoey said firmly.

Alex nodded. The deserted ship frightened him, but he wouldn't let it stop them from discovering what had happened to their friend and her crew. "Everybody, get ready to go aboard."

CHAPTER ELEVEN

DON'T BE CRABBY

The desolate *Dragonfly* lingered in the darkness as Gene tentatively guided their boat closer. It felt like trying to pluck a hair from a walrus's back – one wrong move and all heck would break loose.

Despite appearing empty, the ship had a *presence*. The sense of a slumbering enemy they shouldn't disturb.

Their engine seemed deafeningly loud compared to the stifling silence of the junk ship. Water slapped and sloshed in the narrowing space between their hulls. Once they were in range, Grandpa laid a plank to bridge the vessels. It flexed dangerously under Bridget's bulk as she stepped across to rope the boats together.

"I've been learning my knots," Bridget announced.

"Is that a double carrick bend or two half hitches?" Zoey asked.

Bridget looked confused. "I just made bunny ears and then pulled its whiskers."

Standing beside the plank should have made them feel like a pirate boarding party ready to attack. Instead, Alex felt strangely vulnerable. *The Dragonfly* was shrouded in darkness, heavy shadows offering countless hiding places for whatever awaited them.

Nobody seemed particularly keen to go first.

"Are we ready?" Alex asked. "Where's Anil?"

Zoey pointed to the front of the boat. The plastic tent had been fitted with lanterns, providing enough orange light for Anil and Argosy to each be studying several books at once.

Alex felt another surprising fizz of annoyance as he walked over. "We're about to go aboard."

Anil had been so absorbed in his reading that the interruption made him jump. "Oh, I thought that I might, um...actually stay here?"

"I thought you'd be excited to explore a spooky abandoned ship."

"I am! It's not like I'm scared or anything." Anil spoke quickly, as if trying to chase down any wrong impressions. He glanced at Argosy, who nodded encouragement. "I just think I'm *so* close to finding the cure and we can't afford to lose any time."

"That makes sense." Alex swallowed and nodded a little harder than necessary. It *was* important to find the cure. It would just be weird not to have his friend by his side. "I'm sure we can handle it without you."

Anil winced and opened his mouth to respond but was interrupted by Zoey thrusting a walkie-talkie into his hand. "We'll call if we need backup."

"If I hear any blood-curdling screams, I'll run and help straight away."

"Or we'll run in quite the opposite direction," Argosy added breezily.

Alex glared at the old man, whose moustache was buried in a book bound together by old fishing line. The pair's research was important, but Alex couldn't shake the suspicion that Argosy wasn't quite on their side. If he was trying to take Anil away from them, he would have to be stopped.

He returned to the boarding plank, where Grandpa was handing out wind-up electric torches to the boarding party: Alex, Zoey, Bridget and Gene.

"Keep an eye on Argosy," Alex whispered.

Grandpa nodded firmly. "Aye, I'll watch him like a mantis shrimp."

"Is that a good thing?"

"Best eyesight in the animal kingdom!" Grandpa prodded open one of his eyelids. "A shrimp never misses a thing."

The otters lined up beside Grandpa to offer their support. Everybody else followed Bridget across the plank.

She blocked Gene's path. "You don't have to come, you know."

"I want to help," they said. "Make sure you stay safe."

"Like I need your help," Bridget scoffed. She picked Gene up like they weighed nothing and deposited them on *The Dragonfly*'s deck. "But thank you."

Zoey made retching noises as she climbed over the rail by herself.

They wound their torches. The whirring of the handles reverberated across the deck. Bridget wound fastest, bicep bulging, her torch sputtering to life first. It cast a thin yellow beam that barely illuminated the deck in front of them. The rest of the torches warmed up together, throwing twisted shadows from the rigging and broken lamp-post mast.

"That's weird." Zoey pointed her torch down. The weak light picked out fresh gouges in the boards, long scrape marks punctuated by pin-sized chips and notches. "What leaves marks like that?"

Gene crouched to press their fingers to the wood. "Not people."

Alex shivered. Some calamity had clearly befallen *The Dragonfly*. The crew was missing but the ship hadn't been wrecked like the fishing boats. Kraken flared orange on his shoulder, as if reading his mind and preparing for danger.

Moving in a defensive huddle (which mostly meant using Bridget as a human shield), they aimed their torches in different directions to cover as much of the deck as they could. More signs of a scuffle became evident: ropes of dried seaweed and recycled bed sheets hung limp and unravelled from the rigging; chairs had been knocked over and broken; the contents of rubbish collection bins – cans, tins, plastic bottles – had been spilled across the deck.

They reached the jar of seafire they'd spotted through the eyeglass. Kraken stretched eagerly for the green glow but Alex caught her arm – the deck and its detritus were wet enough to be an infection risk.

Zoey picked up the jar and rolled it between her hands. "Hello?" she called.

Everybody shushed her at once.

"What?!" she protested. "If they're in danger, we need to find them."

"And whatever put them in danger might be trying to find *us*," whispered Bridget.

Zoey stayed quiet after that.

Once they had checked the deck, they moved inside the ship. The darkness grew thicker, their torches seeming only to illuminate a step or two ahead. Zoey held up the jar of seafire, its green glow a little stronger. Still, they were forced to move slowly along a passageway wide enough only for pairs. Alex fell into step alongside Zoey.

"You think they're okay back on the boat?" he whispered.

"Anil can look after himself," Zoey replied. "Well, most of the time."

"I wish he was here with us."

"He's doing the best thing to help the mission. It doesn't matter what we find here if we don't have a cure for the parasites."

Alex knew she was right. There was no sensible reason to take Anil away from his research. It was selfish to want him by his side just because he always had been before.

"I'm worried Argosy might..."

"Corrupt him?" Zoey scoffed. "He's as stubbornly loyal as me. Well, almost."

Alex wished Anil was there to hear the (almost) compliment. It certainly made him feel better.

A doorway led off the passage. Bridget whipped through it, holding her torch like a weapon. Hammocks hung from wooden beams in the room beyond, clothes spilling from chests. Crew quarters, with no sign of the crew.

Clack.

Every light darted in a different direction as they sought the source of the noise.

"What was that?" whispered Gene.

"It sounded like some kind of clack," Zoey observed.

Click-click.

"And that was more of a—"

"We don't need an audio description," said Bridget.

The noises seemed to have come from inside the walls. *The Dragonfly* had always been creaky – inevitable because it was built completely from junk and recycled material. But this was different. It sounded like creatures moving in the bones of the ship.

"Let's keep going," Alex forced himself to say, despite his strong urge to run away.

As they returned to the passageway, their torchlight picked out something at its end. The glint of eyes in the dark. The group huddled together and concentrated their torches on the spot.

"It's just a gross crab," said Bridget.

The crab crouched where the passageway turned a corner into deeper darkness. Its orange and white mottled shell gleamed, claws raised in fearsome symmetry.

"What's it doing?" asked Gene.

In response, Bridget's torch flickered. The light dimmed.

She bashed it against her palm, which only encouraged the bulb to go out completely.

"They're running out of charge!" said Zoey.

The remaining torches dipped together, plunging the hallway into darkness. The faint glow of the seafire isolated them in a shallow pool of green light.

Click-click.

Alex's heart hammered. He recognized the sound now. Crab feet rapping against the wood of the deck and passageways. The whirring sound of winding torches wasn't loud enough to drown it out.

Bridget's torch was first to flutter back to life. Its weak yellow light trickled along the passage, bright enough only to reflect back from multiple sets of beady eyes.

"That looks like a lot more than one crab," said Alex.

The other torches finally lit up. The first crab had now been joined by too many to count. More *click*ed and *clack*ed around the corner, piling up to block the passageway, heavy front claws opening and closing menacingly.

"Do you think they're infected?" asked Zoey.

"I think we can assume—"

Alex was cut off by a hand clamping over his mouth. He stumbled around to find a vent had opened in the wall above his head. Reaching from it, green braids trailing, was Meri.

"They're infected and you definitely want to get out of here," said the captain of *The Dragonfly*.

The crabs seemed to hear. Moving as one, they raised their claws like swords, turned sideways and launched into a scuttling charge.

CHAPTER TWELVE

LOST AND FOUND

Bridget dropped into a squat underneath the vent.

"Climb on me!"

One by one, she boosted everybody up, practically hurling them into the air for Meri to catch and drag to safety. The crabs skittered along the passageway, tumbling over each other in their haste, a frenzied cavalcade of clicking claws.

Alex was last to be launched into the vent. In the torchlight, he saw a square wooden tunnel that burrowed away inside the ship like a rabbit warren. There was just enough space to turn around and squeeze himself beside Meri so they could both reach for Bridget.

When his sister jumped and grabbed their hands, it

almost dragged them out of the vent. Zoey and Gene caught their ankles and pinned them down. Alex thought his arm would pop from its socket.

"You're so heavy," he groaned.

"This isn't the time for compliments!"

Thankfully, Bridget was strong enough to pull herself up quickly. Her legs wriggled inside the vent just as the crabs crowded underneath it, claws snipping at thin air.

"We have to go." Meri slammed the vent cover shut. "They'll climb each other to come after us."

The tunnel was just large enough to shuffle along on their hands and knees. Arms and feet tangled in their haste, heads banging against the low ceiling. Kraken flattened herself on Alex's back while Bridget's broad shoulders meant she had to keep her arms pinned by her sides and kick herself along like a stranded fish.

"Good thing I never skip leg day," she said.

"Keep going!" Meri called ahead. The wavering torchlight showed that Zoey and Gene had reached a corner. "The tunnels go all the way through the ship."

The skirring ricochet of crab feet drummed behind them, claws knocking on wood, as their pursuers spilled inside the vent.

"I knew you'd find a way to stay safe!" said Zoey.

"I had these secret tunnels installed during the rebuild,"

Meri explained as they crawled quickly along. "I thought we might need places to hide. Didn't realize it would be so soon."

"I bet you didn't guess it would be from rabid crabs either," added Alex.

Meri continued as if she wasn't surprised at all. "The storms have been so bad that I knew something was wrong. We rescued the crew of a wrecked fishing boat. They told us the Water Dragon attacked them! None of us believed it until we rescued a second crew who said exactly the same thing."

"The fishermen are here? So that's why the crews were never found!" Alex felt a flush of relief that the dragon hadn't hurt them.

"The storms cut off our communications and whenever we tried to return them to Haven Bay we were attacked by animals. After a few tests, we discovered it was parasites making them behave that way."

"You really should have left the rescuing to the experts," Bridget chastised breathlessly.

"I've just rescued *you*, haven't I?" Meri bit back.

Ahead, Zoey and Gene reached a crossroads with another tunnel branching off in a different direction. The pair hesitated long enough, torches swinging between paths, that everybody else piled into their backs.

"Keep going straight!" Meri directed.

They scrambled onwards. Alex's hands were sore, knuckles blistered and splinters from the wood nipping his skin. His bandage was filthy and unravelling. The air grew hot with panicked breath.

"The crabs came after we rescued a third crew the other night," said Meri. "Enough of them to overwhelm the ship. We managed to escape into the vents and hide. We've had to stay quiet ever since."

"Until we came along and made everything worse," said Alex.

"Only slightly. My call was so scrambled I didn't know if you'd come."

"Of course we did!" called Zoey.

Meri smiled before her expression turned serious again. "I don't think it was rescuing the fishing crews that made the crabs attack. They only appeared right after—"

The tunnel ahead ruptured, the wood splintering and snapping. Crabs poured inside, tumbling over each other like a wave.

"Turn around!" shouted Zoey.

Everybody wriggled awkwardly to face the other way, only to find themselves facing Bridget, shoulders bunched around her ears.

"I can't," she breathed. "You'll have to push me."

Alex and Meri took a shoulder each, knees digging into the floor to drive Bridget backwards as quickly as they could. Zoey and Gene followed closely behind, the frenetic clattering of claws at their heels.

The previously passed fork in the tunnel provided enough space for Bridget to turn around.

"Never tell anybody that happened!" she ordered.

Now she was no longer blocking the torch beams, the light picked out hundreds of beady eyes waiting back the way they had come. Crabs blocked them ahead and behind, swarming closer every second.

"Take the fork!" Meri bellowed.

The dual crab armies crashed together in the mouth of the tunnel just as Zoey and Gene scrambled inside.

"I liked it better when I was at the front," called Zoey.

The air in this stretch of tunnel was cooler on Alex's skin. A faint light glowed somewhere ahead.

"I was trying to lead them away," said Meri.

Sweat dripped into Alex's eyes. "Away from what?"

The vent seemed to appear from nowhere. Alex fell from the tunnel, slamming onto hard ground below. The others – accidentally, he hoped – broke their falls on top of him.

"Ouch," he whimpered.

"Maybe being at the back wasn't so bad," Zoey mused as she rolled off him.

Bright light surrounded them. Alex righted himself to find they had tumbled into a large wooden chamber. Instead of doors or portholes, vents led away in all directions. An assortment of lights – oil lanterns, desk lamps, detached sunbed lids – were lodged onto shelves and alcoves around the walls. People huddled together in puddles of illumination, startled wide eyes fixed fearfully on the new arrivals. Alex recognized some of the missing Haven Bay fishing crews amongst them.

Movement in the middle of the room snatched his attention. High wooden sides held a large pool of water, lapping gently with the movement of the ship. A lion-like, scaly head lifted from the water to regard him.

The baby dragon.

"You're here too!" Alex cheered.

There was no time to celebrate. The sound of scuttling claws swelled. It seemed to echo along every vent, the walls vibrating as it drummed a booming crescendo. *The Dragonfly*'s crew rose slowly from their seats, preparing to fight.

"I think they've found us," said Meri.

Every vent burst open at once and crabs poured into the chamber.

CHAPTER THIRTEEN

THE BATTLE OF *THE DRAGONFLY*

"Protect the dragon!"

Meri's order drew an immediate response. The crew quickly formed into protective rings around the dragon pool. Oars and broken boards were wielded as weapons, while others held shields of dented scrap metal. The dragon lowered itself in the pool to peek over the side with frightened eyes.

Alex was awestruck. Back home, the locals blamed the Water Dragon for everything that went wrong. Here, nobody thought twice about risking their safety to protect its baby.

"Come on!" Zoey grabbed his arm and snapped him into action. They joined the front of the formation, turning to face their scuttling assailants.

The crabs streamed across the floor like spilled paint, seeming to multiply as they surrounded the pool and its protectors on all sides. Pincers clicked together in synchronized rhythm, thundering on the air like a crustacean battle cry.

"I managed to run some tests on infected animals," Meri said. "The parasites can spread from creature to creature as well as through contaminated water. The crabs are going to try and reach the dragon and infect it. We have to keep them away." She lifted her voice so everybody would hear. "But remember: it's not their fault. Don't hurt them unless you have no choice."

"I suspect it might be us getting hurt," said Zoey. She reached into her jacket and took out a walkie-talkie. "Anil, consider this a blood-curdling scream. We need backup right now. Do you read me?"

The walkie-talkie stayed silent. Maybe being so deep inside the ship was blocking the signal.

"We don't need them." Bridget spread her arms wide to encompass as many of the encircling crabs as she could.

Despite being less than half her size, Gene took a stuttering breath and stepped up beside her. "We'll fight together," they said.

"Like we practised?"

Gene nodded. They linked arms, so Bridget could lift

Gene off the ground. Then she arched back as if ready to throw.

"What are you—?" Alex began to ask.

The crabs charged, thousands of armoured feet rattling. Bridget swung Gene forwards in a sweeping arc, feet extended to scatter the crab front line. At the end of the swing, she let Gene go, catching them elegantly in the crook of her other brawny arm to swing again.

"All right, that's the first time they've looked good together," Zoey begrudgingly admitted.

Crabs blitzed the crew from every direction, pinching at feet and clambering up legs, trying to trip people over into the swarm. The crew fought back, using their weapons like brooms to try and push the crabs away. For every crab that was successfully repelled, another managed to break the line, scrambling callously over their fallen comrades.

Alex, Zoey and Meri kicked crabs away, shook them from legs and shoelaces, snatched them off each other to hurl back into the maelstrom. Kraken fired bullets of water from Alex's shoulder, sending crabs spinning away like hockey pucks.

"There's too many of them," Meri groaned, kicking a clinging crab from her trouser leg.

The protective rings of crew were already breaking apart, some dragged forwards, others pushed back to the edge of the pool. The baby dragon swivelled its head in panic, crying out and flinching away if any crab came too close.

Alex had to remind himself that, even though the baby dragon looked to have doubled in size since he saw it last, it was still only a couple of months old. Too young to face such danger, but left with no choice.

Alex shook a crab from his sleeve and climbed up onto the damp edge of the pool.

"It's okay," he told the dragon. Kraken reached out a reassuring arm. "We'll keep you safe."

He dipped a hand into the pool. The salt water seemed to whoosh through his veins, lending him a surge of strength. Still, the pool was shallow, just enough to cover the dragon's armoured back. Alex couldn't use much of the water without leaving the dragon high and dry.

Sea magic flowed from his fingertips. The top layer of the pool lifted up, the dragon briefly wearing it as a necklace. Alex gritted his teeth and *stretched* the water beyond the confines of the pool, heaving it as high as he could. The dragon's mouth dropped open in awe as it watched the water expand.

"Look out!" Alex shouted.

He opened his hand and let the water go. It collapsed like a punctured rain cloud, landing just beyond the crew to rush outwards, a circular wave strong enough to wash the crabs away.

Before the wave could spread out of reach, Alex clenched his fist and hauled the water back. The torrent halted and folded back over itself to form a churning barrier between the regrouping crabs and the crew.

"You didn't quite miss everybody." Black streaks of mascara ran down Bridget's cheeks, water dripping from her sodden hair. She deposited Gene on their soggy feet so they could both shake themselves off.

Meri pushed her braids out of her face. "It's working."

Crabs rushed at the static wave only to be batted back. The crew used the reprieve to collect themselves and re-form the defensive line.

"I can't hold it for long," Alex said through gritted teeth. The wave was spread too wide, with too little water. His grip faltered each time a crab bounced against it.

Something heavy nudged the back of his head. Alex glanced back just as the baby dragon rested its soft-spined chin on his shoulder. Its scales glowed green, lighter than its parent but no less bright. Kraken stroked its muzzle encouragingly.

Slowly, Alex felt its magic mingle with his own. Tentative at first, almost shy, searching for a current it could share. Of the two of them, Alex realized, he was the most experienced with sea magic. He would have laughed if the barrier wave wasn't straining his arms, threatening to break.

The baby was not as strong as the Water Dragon. It and Alex had not yet had the chance to bond. But they were still so much stronger together than apart.

Alex pushed their combined magic out into the water. The wave picked itself up higher, its top foaming and spitting like a feral creature daring the crabs to cross it.

"Any chance you can hold that until the crabs die of old age?" asked Zoey. "I reckon we can outlast them."

Their renewed strength would hold the barrier for a while, but there was still no way to get the baby dragon to safety. They needed to find a way to chase the crabs off the ship all together.

A familiar *ftzz* sound crackled from Zoey's pocket. "Finally!" she said, grabbing the walkie-talkie and pressing it to her ear. "*Now* you answer."

Anil's voice fuzzed through. "*Stand back.*"

"Stand back from what exactly?"

"*Just get away from the—!*"

An explosion rocked *The Dragonfly*. The outer wall of the chamber was broken open, wood splintering as debris flew through the air. Alex was knocked from the side of the pool. He hit the ground hard, Kraken tumbling from his shoulder, and lost his grip on the barrier wave.

A ragged hole had been punched through the side of the ship. Through it, they saw the illuminated deck of Grandpa's boat and the smoking cannon aimed directly at *The Dragonfly*.

"*Oops*," Anil said through the walkie-talkie. "*It wasn't supposed to go off yet.*"

"That's why you should always leave explosions to a professional!" shouted Zoey.

The hole in the boat was high enough in the hull not to swamp them, but seawater still washed inside.

"Stay away from the water!" Alex shouted to the dragon. He searched desperately for Kraken but saw no sign of her.

He summoned as much power as he had left and sculpted another wave from the ankle-deep water. This time he used it to herd crabs towards the hole in the ship. A few were washed out, but there were so many more able to avoid the wave and rush towards the baby dragon.

Zoey tripped over something in the water and almost fell sprawling. The jar of seafire tumbled out of her pocket and floated towards the crabs. As soon as its glow touched their shells they recoiled, raising their claws to cover their eyes.

"That's exactly how Loaf reacted," Zoey said. "I've got an idea!"

"How worried should we be?" asked Alex.

"Just worry about keeping the crabs back until I'm ready!"

She broke away and pushed through the fiercely fighting crew, snatching up the jar of seafire as she went. The lid of a tanning bed had been fixed into the wall, its long, thin bulbs humming with pale blue light. Zoey opened a panel in its electronics. Then she trickled seafire inside.

The light faltered, buzzing harshly as if the bulb might blow. Then the seafire spread through it and the light flushed green. Crabs flinched away, breaking off their attack to escape the glow.

"Seafire repels the infected!" Zoey shouted.

"Open the emergency lighting supply!" Meri shouted.

A cupboard was thrown open and jars of seafire were quickly distributed. The crew poured it into lanterns or simply pushed the jars towards the bewildered crabs. In moments, the whole chamber glowed green.

The crabs retreated, lurching away from one scalding light just to find themselves confronted by another. Only the cannon hole offered an escape and the crabs fought each other to reach it. Alex sent a final wave crashing after them to hasten their exit.

As soon as the last crab was expelled, the crew rushed to begin bailing water and fixing the hole in *The Dragonfly*'s hull.

"Alex!"

He spun around to find Meri collapsed on her knees. She clutched something tightly to her chest; something that was rapidly shifting between different colours.

Kraken.

Alex rushed over and took the octopus to cradle in his arms. Her eyes looked hazy, arms curling in the air as if fighting some invisible enemy.

"She was in the water," Meri said. "From outside."

Alex refused to believe it. "She'll be okay."

He reached along their connection, using the last drops of his sea magic to try and soothe her. But the line was blocked, the power drained away by another force.

Kraken's skin stopped cycling different colours to blaze a bright, angry red. Her arms twitched one last rebuke, before they moved slowly to shield her eyes from the glow of seafire.

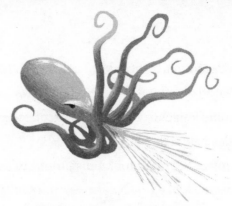

CHAPTER FOURTEEN

SIDE BY SIDE TO SAVE THE WORLD

Magic would not bring her back.

No matter how deeply Alex reached into his well of power, the magic dissipated on contact with Kraken's smouldering red skin. The octopus wrapped her arms tightly around his wrist to try and pull him away, while still covering her eyes against the radiant seafire.

"It can't be too late." Alex choked, voice hitching in his throat.

He rushed towards the baby dragon, holding out Kraken like an offering. Zoey and Meri tried to block his path but he barrelled through them. It took Bridget's size and strength to finally hold him back.

"The dragon can save her," Alex pleaded. "We're strongest together."

Kraken still fought to free herself, spitting water into his face, but Alex held tight.

"She'll infect the dragon," Meri said softly. "We have to keep her away."

The baby dragon lowered its head towards the octopus, eyes large and mournful. Kraken strained to reach it, forcing the dragon to rear back.

Gently, Zoey placed her hands on top of Alex's. "We'll put her somewhere safe. Until we find the cure."

Tears spilled down Alex's cheeks. Briefly, he felt stunned by betrayal. Why wouldn't they help? He wanted to scream out and thrash free of them, just as Kraken kept trying to free herself from him.

Then he saw the truth: it was Kraken who had been betrayed. She had always fought to protect him and Alex had failed to do the same for her.

Resistance drained from him. "Where can we keep her?" he asked.

The dragon lifted itself to its full height. It almost reached the ceiling of the chamber, more of its length coiled inside the depleted pool. Alex couldn't believe how much it had grown. It was at least as big as the Water Dragon had been the first time he'd seen it, trapped inside an abandoned aquarium tank.

Alex allowed his friends to turn him away. The dragon tipped back its head and issued a high-pitched keening that bounced around the chamber. It was calling to its parent. Alex felt its magic skimming across the ocean and knew no reply would come.

As they moved across the chamber, the battle-weary crew was already bailing water through the ragged hole, others gathering backup scrap to patch it up and keep *The Dragonfly* from sinking. Bridget clapped a supportive hand on her brother's shoulder before she and Gene went to help with the repairs.

"*Did we win?*" Anil asked through the walkie-talkie.

"Just get over here," Zoey replied, shutting it off.

Meri led the way. The stairs out of the chamber and the winding hallways of *The Dragonfly* passed in a blur. Alex could only focus on Kraken struggling against him; powerful arms tirelessly trying to prise his fingers apart. Eyes that glared at him without recognition.

Eventually they reached a small cabin with a wide, curved window. The latticed glass offered a view of the treacherous ocean beyond, waves batting the ship side to side. The cabin contained a desk that had been nailed together from two mismatched halves, an upholstered high-backed chair roughly patched with strips of brown tape and an unmade camping cot pushed into the corner. CDs and twists of tin foil, blunted fishing hooks and cat collar bells hung on strings as decoration.

"These are my quarters," said Meri. "She'll be safe here."

Under the window, a half-filled fish tank held a single crab. A brick weighed down the lid to prevent escape. Quickly, Meri whipped away the brick and reached inside to seize the crab, transferring it into a plastic bucket with sides too sheer to climb.

"Put her inside."

Alex tried to drop Kraken into the tank. Zoey and Meri had to peel away her suckering arms before she plopped into the water. The lid was quickly replaced and the brick returned. The blazing octopus slammed herself against the tank, shaking the glass, but couldn't break through. Instead, she squirted a shroud of jet-black ink into the water to hide herself.

"I didn't even know she could do that," Alex said.

"I'm so sorry." Meri reached into her braids and removed an ornately twisted seashell. Sandy red feet and claws emerged from its opening; a pair of shiny black eyes flicking between them all. "I'd do anything to keep Sheldon safe."

Meri's pet hermit crab spotted Kraken and his thin front feelers drooped in sadness.

Alex dropped into the chair, throwing up a cloud of dust.

The others looked to him for what they should do next. But he had nothing to give them. This was more than the usual exhaustion he felt after using his magic. It felt dangerously close to hopelessness.

"Why is it left up to us to save the world?" he asked. "The ocean was being damaged long before we were even born. We didn't cause any of this. But it's still us out here risking our lives to fix it while everybody else sits at home and pretends nothing is happening."

"It's definitely not fair," Zoey said. "But we have power. If we're awesome enough to use it to fight for what's right, we can lead the way for others to do the same."

Alex put his head in his hands. "What if this is too big for us to fight?"

"Meri, maybe you should tell us what happened here," Zoey suggested. "It might help us work out if...how we *are* going to stop all this."

Meri offered Sheldon a shred of lettuce leaf before pushing him back inside her hair. "The baby dragon came to us last night during the storm, right before I managed to get through to you. It was being chased by a whole army of infected sea creatures. We just had time to get it out of the water and into the pool we use for rehabilitating injured animals. Getting it out of the ocean meant it couldn't be infected, but also meant it couldn't use its powers to help us."

That explained why Alex had not been able to find the baby dragon when he sought after it with magic.

"So you couldn't fight off the crabs," said Zoey.

"Exactly. We fended off as many as we could and ran from the rest. But they kept coming." She watched the captive crab in the bucket, which had finally fallen still, as if listening to the story. "We decided to hide instead and hope the crab invasion wouldn't find us. It was going quite well until you showed up."

Zoey winced. "Sorry about that."

"No, I'm glad you found us. We left the trail of seafire hoping you would follow it. The crabs would have got to us eventually. Thanks to you, we kept the baby dragon safe. That gives us a chance of fighting back."

"The baby dragon is still learning its magic. *I'm* still learning. I couldn't even save..." A lump in Alex's throat cut off his words. He and the dragon had combined their magic to fight off the crabs, but their connection wasn't strong enough yet to give them serious power. "If the Water Dragon uses its power against us, there'll be nothing we can do."

"We spoke to the fishermen we rescued," said Meri. "Some of them think the dragon was trying to push them away rather than hurt them."

"That's exactly what Anil said!" Zoey exclaimed. "It's weird to be happy he was right."

"I think the Water Dragon will be strong enough to hold off infection for a while," said Alex. "But I don't know how long it can last."

"Probably not long." Meri was distracted by the crab in the bucket. It had begun to twitch, eyes quivering and legs wobbling drunkenly from side to side. "I managed to study an infected host before we had to hide. Watch."

Finally, the crab dropped onto its belly and its mouth fell open. Black foam poured from inside and spread across the bucket.

"That's disgusting," said Zoey, pushing her face over the lip of the bucket for a closer look.

"The foam is full of microscopic parasites. They breed inside the host and then pour out to search for more animals to infect."

"What about the host?" Alex asked.

"It stays alive." Inside the bucket, the crab slowly got back to its feet. "Still controlled by the parasites and used again to make more eggs. If a single crab can produce this many parasites..."

"The Water Dragon will be the ultimate host." Alex slowly sat forwards in the chair. "It's big enough for millions of parasites to breed. Enough to infect every animal in the ocean."

Meri nodded gravely. "If the parasites are inside the dragon, they'll have laid eggs. We have to cure the dragon before the first batch hatches or they'll take it over for good. There'll be no way for us to stop it."

"I might be able to help with that."

Anil stood in the cabin doorway, a battered book with curling brown pages open in the crook of his arm.

"I wasn't trying to make a dramatic entrance," he said. "I just got lost on the way here."

"Have you found the cure?" Zoey asked.

Anil puffed himself up and cleared his throat, preparing to read.

"It's really just a yes-or-no question," said Zoey.

Anil deflated and handed over the book. "We found the recipe for it."

Alex stood and reached for the book. The page contained a long, handwritten list of ingredients, most of which he didn't recognize. But it didn't matter. This was the cure! It could save Kraken and Loaf. It could save the Water Dragon. It could save the *world*.

"You did it," he said.

Anil smiled. "Once I found the 1743 passenger lists from the ferryman's guild, it was easy enough to cross-reference them with—"

Alex cut him off by pulling him into a hug. Embers of hope glowed inside Alex – maybe there really was a chance. If he hadn't been so happy, he'd have felt embarrassed for ever doubting his friend. "You really have found the thing you're best at."

"This is really nice but also I can't breathe."

Alex let him go. Meanwhile, Meri had opened a cupboard and was riffling through bottles of powder and tincture, crystals and bundles of dried leaves.

"I know everything apart from that last ingredient." Meri squinted at the word. "*Zircongris?*"

"I've never heard of it either." Zoey frowned. "Maybe it's not that important. If we have everything else, maybe we can substitute it."

Alex tried to read the list but his vision blurred with fatigue. Using so much magic had left him feeling hollowed out. "We won't let the dragon fall." He had failed Kraken – he would do whatever it took not to fail the Water Dragon. "But right now, I need to rest."

"You can have my first mate's cabin next door," said Meri. "We'll work together and brew the cure by the time you wake up."

Zoey nodded. "Kraken will be better before you know it."

The octopus still blazed red, as if trying to boil the water away. Alex rested his fingers against the glass.

I'll save you, he thought, hoping somehow it might get through. *Then we'll be side by side to try and save the world again.*

CHAPTER FIFTEEN

TECHNICALLY NOT DRAGON POOP

The cure looked like a smoothie of seafire, algae and seagull droppings. The chunky liquid glared sickly green, black lumps clinging to the inside of the glass vial. When Alex turned it upside down, it hardly moved.

"Have you tried it yet?" he asked, rubbing sleep from his eyes. Thin morning light pushed through the wide window of Meri's quarters.

Zoey pulled a face. "Yeah, it tastes terrible."

"I meant have you tried it on any infected animals?"

"Oh. Not yet. We only finished it just before you woke up."

Alex had slept like a log of driftwood: deeply enough not to be awakened, though dreams tossed him on tumultuous

133

waves. He remembered seeing himself alongside the baby dragon, watching helplessly as a tsunami thundered towards them, the water twisting into a gaping mouth to swallow them up.

It hadn't left him feeling particularly well rested, but it had been enough to chase away the gloom of the night before.

Zoey and Meri looked worse. Heavy bags hung under their eyes. Their clothes were splashed with unidentifiable stains and crusts of powder. A hole in Zoey's overalls looked suspiciously like a burn mark. She covered it up when she caught him looking.

"I'm sorry about what I said last night," Alex said.

Zoey smiled sympathetically. "You've given enough pep talks in the past to balance it out. And you were right – it's *not* fair we have to deal with this. But I'm not ready to give up yet."

"Me neither! We still haven't identified zircongris." Anil looked tired too, as if he had stayed up all night searching the archive. Alex was beginning to feel guilty for sleeping.

"But we've done our best without it," said Meri.

Zoey rubbed her eyes with both fists. "Now we just need to test it."

She glanced at Kraken in the fish tank. The brick had held, the lid still secure. The octopus hovered near the glass as if eavesdropping on their conversation.

"Not on her," Alex said. "The crab."

The bucket had been filled with enough water to keep the crab submerged without it being able to escape. Carefully, Meri removed the stopper from the vial and tipped it. The cure hardly moved. Only a firm shake sent a glob splashing into the bucket.

It fizzed in the water, dissolving slowly to turn it a faint green. A smell like burnt seaweed filled the air. The crab hardly seemed to notice.

"How do we know if it's worked?" asked Alex.

Anil thrust his hand into the bucket. The crab immediately pinched one of his fingers and held on tight. "It's not cured!" Anil cried, flapping his hand to try and dislodge the crab.

"I'd have done that whether I was infected or not." Zoey picked up a jar of seafire from the desk and pushed it towards the crab. It instantly released Anil's finger and tumbled back into the bucket, where it shielded its eyes with its claws. Minutes passed and nothing changed.

Alex tried to keep the disappointment from his face. He knew how hard they had tried. "It didn't work."

Zoey and Meri sagged. Before, they had looked tired; now they looked exhausted.

"We'll try again," Meri vowed.

"But without the missing ingredient..." Zoey rubbed her eyes and shook her head.

"I believe I know exactly what you're missing."

Erasmus Argosy stood in the cabin doorway, peering at them over the top of his glasses.

"I wish people would knock instead of making dramatic announcements when they enter my quarters," Meri muttered.

"Zircongris is one of the rarest substances on the planet," Argosy said, too intent on his theatrical entrance to be deterred. "Nobody has possessed any for hundreds of years. Not even my family's illustrious and voluminous collection has been able to acquire the slightest—"

"I really don't mean to be rude," Zoey said, rudely interrupting, "but are you about to spend a long time blustering about history and showing off your knowledge when you could just tell us the answer really quickly?"

Argosy adjusted his glasses, moustache twitching. "Possibly."

"Then maybe just skip ahead and tell us *why* it's so hard to find."

"Because," Argosy sniffed, still treating himself to a climactic pause, "it can only be found inside the Water Dragon."

Everybody's jaws dropped open at once.

Anil was the first to recover. "*Inside?*"

"In its bowels, if you must know."

"Gross," Zoey said, beaming.

"Zircongris is a digestive by-product said to have remarkable magical properties." Argosy produced a page torn from a book, creases suggesting it had been folded up and hidden. It showed an illustration of a soft, bulb-like shape growing from a rock. "When there were more dragons, small amounts of it could be obtained. They would occasionally...excrete enough to be collected."

"So it's dragon poop?" Zoey asked.

Argosy shuddered. "Not technically, no."

Alex fixed him with a cold stare. "Why didn't you tell us this last night?"

"Why didn't you tell *me*?" Anil asked, sounding wounded.

"Because I hoped your cure might work without it!" Argosy protested. "We have about as much chance of obtaining zircongris as we do of teaching the dragon imperial weights and measures."

"There might not be as many as there used to be, but we still have two Water Dragons we could get it from," Alex said.

Nobody answered. Instead, they eyed each other nervously, each waiting for somebody else to speak.

"You haven't shown him?" Argosy finally asked.

Alex spoke through gritted teeth. "Shown me what?"

It was shockingly cold on deck. A sharp wind pushed straight into Alex's bones and made him shiver. The sun was hidden behind featureless grey cloud like slate, the ocean reflecting it blankly. Light rain misted his skin.

The Dragonfly was still, *Dorothea* moored alongside. The otters appeared at the rail and chirruped across a greeting. For some reason, they were now wearing individually knitted woolly hats.

Grandpa appeared alongside them. "Sorry we en't come over to see yer," he called. "We're keepin' this boat as quarantine so these lads don't get infected."

Someone on the crew must have told Grandpa what had happened to Kraken. Guilt lanced through Alex's belly. "Keep them safe," he called back.

"Why do they have hats now?" Zoey asked.

"It's lonely over 'ere and I got bored." Grandpa reached down towards his feet and lifted up Chonkers. The cat glared out from underneath a knitted admiral's hat, a pea coat with golden embroidery fitted over her back.

The Dragonfly's crew were busy about their duties, clambering around the rigging to manage the bed-sheet sails and scrubbing the scrap-wood deck. A few boards were missing, used to mend the hole in the hull and keep the ship seaworthy. At the prow, Bridget and Gene took turns looking through an eyeglass. Alex followed their gaze but saw nothing except a bank of black cloud low on the horizon.

Bridget smiled when she spotted him. "How you feeling, little bro?"

"What are you looking at?" Alex asked in return, reaching for the eyeglass. A strange sense of dread was beginning to weigh on him. Magic blew on the wind, coming from the direction of the cloud bank.

The dark horizon leaped at him through the eyeglass lens. The cloud bank was actually a storm. Lightning seethed and snapped at the choppy water. Rain poured in sheets. No ship would dare sail into such weather. Were they watching it to make sure they didn't stray too close?

"Keep watching," Bridget said.

A column of cloud swirled and broke apart. Beyond it reared the monumental head of the Water Dragon, cavernous mouth agape in a silent roar. Lightning licked its scales and rain lashed the scarred armour plates along its back. A moment later, the storm closed around it again.

Alex lowered the eyeglass, heart thundering in his chest. He was scared for the dragon, desperate to sail into the storm and help. But, for the first time since he had discovered it, Alex realized he was also scared *of* the dragon. A primal, guilty part of him simply wanted to run.

"The Water Dragon has closed itself inside a storm wall so nothing can get close," Meri said. "We're not sure if the dragon is keeping us away for our safety or if the parasites know we're coming and want to shut us out."

Alex kept his eyes on the distant storm. "Everybody knew about this?"

"We sailed within range around daybreak."

"We didn't want to disturb you," added Zoey.

Alex took a deep breath and waited for his heartbeat to stop pounding in his ears. He couldn't let himself get overwhelmed. "You should have told me straight away."

"I didn't want to wake you up because..." Zoey trailed off and looked away.

"You've always told me exactly what you're thinking," Alex said, trying to smile. "Why stop now?"

"Because every new bit of information makes it feel more impossible," she said, eyes growing wet as she met his gaze again. "Because I'm beginning to worry we can't win."

Alex took a step back as if he had been struck. Zoey had always been the one who believed they could overcome the steepest odds. Who told them they could accomplish anything if they believed in it and fought hard enough. Alex would never have got this far without her indomitable faith.

The odds had stacked against them so quickly. The ocean – the place where he should have felt safest, most in control

– was now his enemy. If the parasites were coordinating to stop them, anything could attack at any moment.

"I used to be so scared of the water," Alex said.

Zoey snorted. "I remember. You wouldn't even go near a rock pool."

He sighed. "Getting over that fear was the hardest thing I've ever done. When I finally discovered my power, finally felt at ease with the water...it was such a *relief.* It was like being released from a cell I hadn't known I was trapped inside."

"I also would have been happy to receive awesome superpowers," noted Zoey.

Anil nodded. "Same."

"I know it all seems impossible. But I have to keep believing we can win," Alex said. "Because I won't go back to being scared."

"Is this a *the harder the fight, the harder we fight* kind of pep talk?" Zoey asked.

Alex managed to smile. "I probably sound like a broken record."

"To be fair, recent adventures have really helped you nail your inspirational speeches."

"Practice makes perfect."

"Can I add to this stirring moment by showing off for a second?" asked Meri.

Zoey grinned. "That's usually what I do."

"I've learned from the best. Before all of this happened, *The Dragonfly* was dedicated to cleaning up the ocean. We picked up litter, recycled everything we could, washed animals who were covered in oil."

Meri gestured to the equipment stowed around the deck: bins full of plastic bottles and tin cans, reels of old fishing nets, barrels of oily water washed from animals and safely stored away from the waves.

"The whole crew knows we can't fix the problem on our own," Meri continued. "We keep doing it because even the smallest effort still makes a difference. And if enough people try instead of thinking it's too late to help, then maybe we really can make things better."

"We still have sea magic on our side," Alex said. "But magic alone won't be enough to save the ocean. Zoey, why did you keep inventing things after I discovered my powers?"

"Because my inventions are amazing and I wanted to prove it to everyone."

Alex raised an eyebrow.

"Fine." Zoey smiled. "Because I've always known that the only way we can really win is to equip people who don't have superpowers – which, by the way, is *literally* everyone else – so they can make a difference too."

"Like me," said Meri.

Anil threw his hand in the air. "And me!"

"For the record, I've always totally known I was making a difference, so this whole pep talk was pointless for me," noted Bridget.

"Everybody here has made a difference," Alex said. "Enough to believe we can win now."

Last night, he had come close to despair. Now he wanted to fight.

"Can we extract zircongris from the baby dragon?" Zoey asked. Her eyes flicked from side to side, which Alex knew meant her despondency had cleared and ideas – both brilliant and bonkers – were racing through her mind once again.

Argosy had hung back from the group. He shook his head as he stepped closer. "It's too young to have developed any yet. Look, all this sprightly talk is very, uh...what's the word? Rousing. But the fact remains—"

Zoey cut him off. "Can we get close enough to the dragon to surgically remove some?"

Meri shook her head. "It would be dangerous, for us and the dragon. Plus I'm not sure we've got the tools for dragon surgery."

"The zircongris is in its bowel, right?" asked Anil. "What if we mix up a dragon laxative and—?"

"I'm going to stop you there," said Zoey.

"There's only one option."

Alex braced himself before he continued speaking. He wasn't used to being the one who came up with the most ridiculous idea. As soon as he said it aloud there could be no taking it back. But he knew there was no other choice.

He gazed out towards the raging storm wall. "We have to go inside the Water Dragon."

CHAPTER SIXTEEN

MONSTER AVENGERS

They had hatched plenty of implausible plans before, but this was by far the most dangerous.

"Even *I* think this is ridiculous," Zoey said. "And literally every idea I come up with is objectively hazardous."

Anil nodded enthusiastically. "You've actually managed to outdo her."

Thankfully, these comments were made as they began preparations to carry out the plan despite its extremely perilous nature. The Water Dragon was the biggest Alex had ever seen it. The storm wall reached from the clouds to the surf, the dragon looming like a skyscraper behind it. Big enough for them to go inside, harvest the zircongris needed to formulate a proper cure and then deliver it to the site of the infection before the parasites could hatch several million babies.

Easy.

The core group – including Meri, Bridget and Gene – returned to the chamber at the heart of *The Dragonfly*. The baby dragon remained confined to its isolation pool there. A patch filled the hole in the hull and the floor had been painstakingly mopped and dried. Seafire lanterns burned as protection against any parasites that might remain.

The baby dragon rested its chin on the edge of the pool, keening from somewhere deep in its throat. Magic prickled on Alex's skin. The dragon was still calling for its parent, refusing to give up even though there was no answer.

"I managed to study the baby dragon a little while we were all hiding down here," Meri said.

She climbed onto the edge of the pool and offered a flat hand to the dragon. It eyed her warily before nudging closer, seeking reassurance in her touch. Alex was surprised by a pang of jealousy. What if somebody else forged a bond with the baby dragon before him?

"I was examining how its armour plates hadn't yet fully fused together," Meri continued, reaching for the dragon's back. The curved plates of armour formed a patchwork of grey and green scales waiting to harden. A narrow channel ran down their middle so the dragon could grow into their shape.

Anil whipped out his notepad and pen to scribble notes.

Meri stroked the length of the baby dragon's serpentine back, making it close its eyes and bare its teeth in satisfaction. It reminded Alex of when he scratched the otters between their ears. Carefully, Meri slipped her fingers under the edge of one of the armour plates. It lifted easily as if on a hinge.

A pair of elongated, symmetrical holes twitched and flared underneath like nostrils.

"A blowhole!" Anil exclaimed.

Zoey pressed forwards for a closer look. "If the adult Water Dragon has one too…"

"Then it's our way inside," Alex finished.

Strangely, he had to stifle a laugh. The plan should have been shot down immediately as impossible. Instead, they might just have found a way to make it work.

That left them no choice but to give it a try.

"Any idea what we'll find after we get in there?" he asked.

"The grossest holiday of all time." Zoey chuckled, then glanced guiltily at the baby dragon. "No offence."

"Based on what Argosy told us, the zircongris shouldn't be too far from the point of entry," Meri said. "The problem is, from studying Kraken and the crabs, I've worked out that the centre of infection is the brain. So after you've got the last ingredient for the cure from the dragon's bowel you'll have to travel all the way up its body to administer it."

"The records suggest the cure should kill off all the parasite eggs," said Anil. "Then the live parasites too, but that takes longer. And if the eggs hatch, there'll be too many for the cure to be totally effective. So we have to get up to the brain in time to destroy the eggs before they hatch and spill out into the ocean."

Zoey nodded. "Then get the heck out of there while the cure finishes off any live parasites."

"And frees the Water Dragon from their power," Alex concluded.

The baby dragon flicked its eyes between them as if following the conversation. Hopefully it understood enough to realize they would risk everything to save its parent.

Alex faced his friends. "I know I just made a big deal about us sticking together to fight against impossible odds and all the usual stuff, but I won't force anybody to come with me."

Zoey huffed indignantly. "Like I'm going to miss the opportunity to crawl around the disgusting guts of a giant sea monster." She winced and bowed her head to the baby dragon. "Again, no offence."

"And there's no way I'm missing the chance to map the dragon's anatomy." Anil tapped the notes he'd already made. "Plus, imagine what kind of treasure the dragon must have swallowed in the last thousand years or so!"

Alex smiled and opened his mouth to thank them. A hand in his face from Zoey stopped him short.

"I know that look. You're going to be all sappy and grateful." She grimaced. "It makes it much harder to hold all of this against you later when things inevitably go wrong."

"I'll just take your support for granted instead."

Zoey smiled serenely. "That's all we ask."

Meri hopped down from the pool edge and pulled a walkie-talkie from her braids. "I'll stay on *The Dragonfly* and watch for any sign that the dragon is losing its fight against the parasites. Then we can pick you up when you come out."

A scoff from behind reminded Alex that Bridget and Gene were with them. Now his sister stepped forwards.

"I stayed quiet in case you expected *me* to go inside the dragon." She shivered at the prospect. "But you don't seem to have even thought about how you'll get there in the first place. You might have noticed the *massive storm* around it?"

"I was hoping you might recklessly pilot a boat to get us close enough," Alex said.

Gene opened their mouth to protest at the same moment as Bridget said, "I'm listening."

"Even working together, the baby dragon and me aren't strong enough to stop that storm."

Tentatively, Alex reached towards the dragon. It considered his hand for a moment before bowing to nuzzle against his fingers. The baby's scales felt softer than its parent's. The spines under its chin bent like reeds in a breeze. It was so young.

Still, magic crackled where they touched. Alex felt the potential of their combined power. There seemed to be an empty space inside him where he was sure a connection would form.

"We only need to be strong enough to punch *through* the storm," Alex continued. "Together, we'll protect *The Dragonfly* long enough to create a diversion so the landing party can sneak up on the Water Dragon in the *Dorothea*."

Everybody looked to everybody else for objection, but there were none. Only Gene appeared appropriately horrified.

"Are your plans always this impulsive and half-baked?" they asked.

Zoey tilted her head in thought. "Yeah, pretty much."

It would be a race to save the Water Dragon before the parasite eggs hatched. Everybody hurried off to get ready.

As Alex made his way up towards deck so he could relay the plan to Grandpa, Erasmus Argosy stepped from the shadows and pulled him into a quiet storage room.

"This is madness," he hissed. "I've never heard such a preposterous plan in all my life."

Alex crossed his arms firmly over his chest. The old man would only try and talk him into a less effective idea that would take too long. "Instead of eavesdropping, you could have offered a better plan."

"I have one." Argosy sighed and pinched the bridge of his nose. "You need a plan B. In case you're not able to cure the Water Dragon."

He reached inside his jacket and brought out a small glass vial. Pitch-black liquid brimmed inside. The vial's stopper was secured in place by leather thongs.

Icy cold spread down Alex's spine. "What is it?"

"Poison. A most deadly toxin." Argosy pushed the bottle towards him. "You must administer it to the Water Dragon if it cannot be saved."

Alex staggered backwards. "You want me to *poison* the dragon?"

"Only if you must!" Sweat beaded on Argosy's forehead and misery dragged at his expression. "An infected Water Dragon is too dangerous. Not only will it spill enough parasites into the ocean to compromise it for ever, but the dragon's powers will fall under the parasites' control. It would be the most destructive force this planet has ever seen. Nobody – not even you – would be able to stand against it."

Hundreds of years ago, the enraged Water Dragon had taken a bite out of the coastline. Alex had seen it summon storms and bend hundreds of sea creatures to its will. Now it was bigger and stronger than ever.

Alex stared at the vial and shook his head. It was unthinkable. There would be no way to forgive himself if he had to do it.

The thought stopped him cold. If he *had* to do it.

Argosy was right. He and the baby dragon stood no chance against its parent if the Water Dragon lost its battle against the parasites. But if the dragon was gone, there might still be a chance to retake control of the ocean.

"The dragon would become nothing more than a mindless monster," Argosy said.

Alex squeezed his jaw. "We'll do anything we can to prevent that happening. This would be the last resort."

Argosy nodded sadly. "That's all I ask."

Slowly, fighting every urge in his body, Alex reached out and took the vial of poison.

CHAPTER SEVENTEEN

BEYOND THE STORM WALL

High wind battered *The Dragonfly*, slicing through the myriad gaps in the assembled junk and raising its voice in a whistling wail, as if the ship cried out against the storm's assault.

"Reef the sails!" Meri called.

The crew scrambled to obey, even as the ship heeled back on the crest of a mountainous wave, forcing everybody to hold tight wherever they could. The patchwork sails rolled up to leave only a little material bulging gluttonously with wind.

"I really hope we did a good job rebuilding this ship!" Anil cried, clinging to the rail as *The Dragonfly* pitched forwards to careen down the other side of the wave.

"My dad led the work!" Zoey shouted back. "This ship can withstand anything!"

Alex hoped she was right. The storm wall loomed ahead. Through the telescope, it had seemed enormous. Up close, it was like the world coming to an end. Black cloud had tumbled from the sky to ride the roiling sea. Lightning crawled through it like insects, thunder rattling the bones of the ship. The sparking light cast fleeting silhouettes of the dragon inside the storm, its colossal body lifted from the ocean as if trying to escape the tainted water.

Rain lashed the deck. Alex barely noticed it soaking his clothes and skin. The immense power of the Water Dragon weighed on him far heavier. He was so *small* compared to its boundless strength, a blinking buoy tossed by a hurricane.

"I never thought I'd have to fight against the dragon," he said.

Zoey and Anil each put a hand on his shoulders. "At least you don't have to do it alone."

Their support gave Alex the courage to catch Meri's attention and nod. Instantly, she bellowed another order to her crew.

"Bring up the dragon!"

A heavy *thunk* resounded through the deck. A seam opened in the wood and wide hatch doors were cranked open. The crew dropped ropes inside before taking their places at levers and pullies. A signal was given from below and the ropes went taut as the crew heaved on them.

The baby dragon's head appeared first, scaly brow furrowed and pearlescent eyes fixed as it endured the indignity. A cradling harness had been fitted around its middle, the dragon's sinuous body sagging over it. The otters huddled on the dragon's back.

Wind caught the apparatus and made the ropes creak and lurch. As soon as it was clear of the hatch, the ropes were fixed in place, suspending the dragon low enough for Alex to reach up and touch it when the time came. Plastic sheets were raised to protect it from sea spray.

"Sorry about this," Alex said. "It's the only way to use your power without you going in the ocean."

The baby dragon huffed bitterly, before fixing its nervous gaze on the fury of the fast-approaching storm wall.

"I've come up with code names for this mission," Zoey said.

Alex steeled himself. "How insulting are they?"

"You will be Invasive Invertebrate," she informed him, before looking to Anil. "And you will be Trembling Tapeworm."

Anil opened his mouth to protest before deciding it

wasn't worth it. "And what should we call you?"

Zoey brushed her fringe from her eyes and puffed out her chest. "You may refer to me as Doctor Dragon."

A stinging squall of wind almost knocked her off her feet. A barrel bounced away along the deck, narrowly avoiding some crew, while pieces broke off the rigging and were whipped overboard.

"Make sure the rest of the barrels are properly secured!" Meri barked. "The last thing we need is oil leaking everywhere."

The storm wall obliterated any distinction between sea and sky. Its supernatural force threatened to grind *The Dragonfly* to pieces. The ship peaked over another wave, slanting almost vertically before it hurtled down the other side like a roller coaster drop.

"Take in the last of the sails!" Meri ordered, lifting her voice over the ceaseless roar of the wind. She looked to Alex. "I think it's time."

Alex stood underneath the baby dragon. It watched the storm doubtfully, but its scales ignited all the same, a beacon of light in the rapidly descending darkness.

Everything around them was soaked, the relentless stinging spray deluging the deck, rain buffeting the ship with every squall. The plastic sheets kept the baby dragon dry, but Alex could simply be on deck and connect to the water. He stood as firmly as possible and pressed a hand to the belly of the dragon.

This time, their power combined easily. Channels forged during the crab attack allowed magic to flow freely. The baby dragon's scales blazed green and the darkness of the storm retreated before the light.

Alex held the magic inside himself, crashing around his bones and muscle like a raucous wave. The wall of cloud and lightning would hit the ship at any moment. The tossing waves and scathing spray were difficult enough to grasp. But an unseen force weighed against him too, trying to push him away. It would block any attempt to dismantle the storm.

"Everything okay?" Meri asked tensely.

In seconds, *The Dragonfly* would be ripped to pieces. Alex squeezed his eyes shut. The baby dragon appeared in his mind, their thoughts and feelings colliding. It saw itself winding around its parent, infinitely smaller, its power nothing more than a fleeting spark against such a mighty force.

You're not that strong yet, Alex thought, trusting the baby dragon would hear him. *But you're strong enough to save it.*

"Hurry up!" shouted Zoey.

The clamour of the advancing storm and the panicked

voices of the crew sounded far away. Alex held the baby dragon firmly in his mind and remembered rescuing the Water Dragon from the aquarium, fighting side by side to aid its escape, battling to save the dragon egg. The baby dragon still had so many memories to make with its parent.

It roared its longing and fury, and their magic surged in harmony. Power cascaded through Alex and he thrust his hand towards the storm wall.

Magic streamed from his fingers and punctured the storm wall just as the bow of *The Dragonfly* reached it. The cloud swirled open a portal to admit the ship.

The power came from deeper than Alex had ever reached, gushing as if an ancient well had been tapped, forcing his body rigid as it poured out. Magic bored through the cloud to clear a tunnel. Lightning licked around the ship, forking fingers feeling for the mast, but Alex and the baby dragon batted it away. Their magic twined together, strong enough to carve fleeting safety from the vengeful maelstrom.

See! Alex thought.

Above him, the baby dragon rumbled, scales flaring brighter as it revelled in these newly plumbed depths of power. The otters chirruped in celebration.

"We're nearly through!" Anil shouted.

The entire crew had halted where they stood to marvel

at their passage through the storm. Now their necks craned upwards as they emerged on the other side.

The Water Dragon rose from the ocean like a monumental spire of coiled rock. The armour plates across its back, pocked and scarred over centuries, looked like a chain of islands hoisted into the sky. The dragon's proud head was high enough to be swathed in cloud, the long spines on its chin trailing like frozen rain. Next to it, *The Dragonfly* seemed little more than a toy.

Alex hardly believed that such tiny parasites could threaten such a mighty, majestic creature. But he saw the unnatural rigidity of the Water Dragon's posture, its usually flexile coils locked tight, scales a ruddy, ashen white. Every last drop of its magic was being spent on keeping the parasites from fully taking over.

The baby dragon wailed at the sight, reaching for its parent with its magic. The connection was still there – enough for them both to feel the Water Dragon's anguish, revulsion and despair at what ailed it. But the baby dragon's desperate cry of love was blocked by the dark force of the parasites.

"Time to go," Alex said, turning to Meri. "Get the dragon's attention and keep it distracted for as long as you can."

Meri reached inside her jacket and removed a bright red, snub-nosed flare gun. "I think I can manage that."

"I remember the days when I got to use the cool flare gun." Zoey pouted.

"You're about to go inside an ancient sea monster," Anil said. "If that's not exciting enough, you might have a problem."

Before he followed them to the stern of the ship, Alex reached up to touch the baby dragon again. "You can keep everybody safe without me," he said aloud. "Show the Water Dragon how strong you are."

The baby dragon's undeveloped ruff inflated just enough to make it look like it had swallowed a volleyball. It fixed its eyes on its parent, scales glowing brighter as its magic swelled.

A rope ladder had been suspended from the back rail of the ship. The *Dorothea* tossed in *The Dragonfly*'s wake. Bridget and Gene were busy preparing to cast off, Grandpa holding on tight.

"Ready?" Alex called from above.

Bridget waved for them to board. One by one, they climbed down the ladder, practically falling into the boat as it rocked on the waves.

Zoey went straight to a heavy backpack already loaded into the boat, the contents tinkling and clanking as she checked through.

"Did you bring her?" Alex asked.

Bridget produced a small, clear bag filled with water.

Kraken was furled inside, skin still flaming red, arms wrapped tightly about herself. "I gave her that natural sedative Meri made." She wrinkled her nose. "It smelled like unwashed weightlifting gloves."

"Yer sure it's a good idea to take her with you?" asked Grandpa.

"This way we can cure her as soon as we have the zircongris." Alex gently took the bag and passed it to Zoey, who fitted it securely into her backpack before shouldering it. The backpack was enormous and the outside bulged in strange shapes. Wires trailed from a frayed hole that looked like it had been deliberately picked open.

Alex, Zoey and Anil lined the rails, while Bridget and Gene finished preparing the *Dorothea*. The conditions had been rough on the much larger *Dragonfly*. The smaller boat reeled and see-sawed like it might capsize every time it met a wave.

"We won't fire up the engine until we know the dragon is distracted." Gene took their position at the wheel. "Do you remember your sailing lessons?"

Bridget reached for the rope that secured them to *The Dragonfly*. "I remember the bits that weren't boring."

"And which bits were those?"

"Mainly all the things you told me not to do."

Bridget tugged the knot apart. The boat was seized

instantly by a gust of wind that snapped them from behind *The Dragonfly*. A wave washed over the side and threatened to swamp them. Gene fought to turn the boat head on to the waves while Zoey and Anil started bailing.

The wind carried a cry from *The Dragonfly*. Moments later, its sails unfurled. Eager wind filled them and the ship swerved away on a path that would take it in front of the dragon. The flare shot up from the deck, fired into the face of the wind so its smoky trail held straight before it popped into pink fire.

In answer, a tremendous rumbling fell from the sky.

"Is that thunder?" asked Anil.

Alex peered upwards. "I don't think so."

The Water Dragon's tremendous head dropped out of the clouds. The rumbling growl ran the entire length of its body, waves rippling where it broke the surface. Briefly, Alex recognized how the Haven Bay locals saw the dragon: a monster.

As soon as the dragon saw *The Dragonfly*, waves kicked up around it, herding the ship back towards the storm wall.

"We were right," Alex said. "It was only ever trying to push people to a safe distance."

He had *known* the Water Dragon wouldn't hurt anybody unless it had completely lost control. There was still time to make sure that never happened.

"It's looking the other way," Gene said, gripping the wheel tightly.

Bridget fired up the engine and immediately pushed it to full throttle, sending them skipping wildly over the waves. Gene wrestled to aim the boat directly at where the dragon's body emerged from the water.

"Now *this* is sailing!" Bridget cheered, wrapping her arms around Gene to stay upright.

Grandpa clung to the rail for dear life. "I'm startin' to think I've failed in my role as responsible adult."

"Get us as close as you can," shouted Alex.

The Water Dragon's tail was anchored in the swirling water. The first flattened coil was almost flush with the surface, providing a potential landing platform. Bridget and Gene worked in accidental balance to take them closer, Bridget using the engine to race recklessly forwards, Gene using the wheel to meet the waves and approach at an angle that wouldn't dash them to pieces.

"It's going to be too far to jump," Alex said, watching the restless waves crash against the grey-and-green hump of the dragon's back.

Bridget considered the gap between the boat and the dragon, glanced at each of her arms in turn and then ran her eyes over the boarding party.

"I can throw you," she said.

"That seems to be your answer to everything these days," Gene noted.

Zoey stepped up as first volunteer, fighting to keep a smile off her face. "It's a sacrifice I'm willing to make."

Once the boat was as close as it could get, Gene held them steady against the fierce waves. Bridget gripped Zoey by a wrist and plucked an ankle to lift her off the ground as if she weighed nothing.

"You should eat more protein."

Bridget swung the smaller girl back once, twice, and then let her go. Zoey flew through the air, arms and legs flailing, before landing on the dragon's back.

"Doctor Dragon has landed!" she called.

Anil was launched next, landing hard on the armour plate, Zoey waiting to safely gather him up.

Bridget extended a burly arm. "Your turn, little bro."

"You're enjoying this, aren't you?"

"Throwing my brother and his annoying friends at a dragon?" She shrugged. "I don't hate it."

Grandpa squeezed his shoulder. "Be careful."

Bridget took Alex's wrist and snatched a leg from under him. The world flipped as she wound up the swing, definitely a little harder than she had for the others.

"Just go limp!" Bridget shouted, which only made him tense up further.

He arced through the bottom of the final swing and felt his sister's grip shift to release him. Before she could, a wild gust of wind tipped her off balance and Bridget stumbled, letting him go too late.

The throw sent him high into the air and the wind snatched him. It carried him towards where the dragon's body coiled up and away from the water. Alex collided with unyielding scales and scrabbled for grip, water making them slick. The angle of the dragon's body was steep and he tumbled down its back.

Head over heels, elbows and knees bashing against scales, the churning ocean rushing up fast from below. There was nothing Alex could do to stop the fall.

Hands caught his wrists and held tight. Pain lanced through his shoulders as he came to a halt, legs kicking in search of a foothold. Alex looked up to see Zoey and Anil reaching from beneath an armour plate, each holding one of his arms.

"We found the blowhole," Anil shouted over the whistling wind.

"Ready to go inside the dragon?" asked Zoey.

Apparently, it was a rhetorical question. They wrenched him up, and this time he fell into darkness.

CHAPTER EIGHTEEN

ENTER THE DRAGON

Air rushed in Alex's ears as he slipped down a curving, soft-walled tunnel. At first, he thought it was just the wind and the speed of descent. Then he caught its rhythm – air sucking downwards, then blowing back up the tunnel – and realized it was *breathing*.

He was falling *inside* the Water Dragon.

Alex flailed in panic. The walls of the tunnel were strangely sticky. He was sliding through gunk, which was thickening under his legs, slowing his descent enough to straighten up and regain control. A faint green light below his feet silhouetted his friends falling ahead of him.

"Brace yourselves!" Alex shouted.

Anil whimpered. "Why?"

"Because at the bottom of steep tunnels there's usually a—"

Zoey and Anil dropped out of sight. The blowhole ended abruptly and Alex's stomach lurched as he fell into empty air. Grey water rushed up from below. Alex threw out his hands to summon air bubbles around his friends' faces before they splashed down.

Except there was no splash. The water didn't swallow him up. It cratered softly underneath him, thick and cloying like treacle. Alex began to sink into the liquid as if being absorbed. It glooped around his legs, sticky strings stretching from his arms when he tried to wrench them clear.

Zoey floundered beside him, fruitlessly poking at the air bubble covering her nose and mouth. Alex slapped the surface of the gunk and both their bubbles popped.

"Go flat on your back and kick," she said, pointing behind him.

An outcrop of jagged rock rose from the swamp. Alex stopped struggling and flattened himself evenly so he was no longer sinking. Then, carefully, he kicked both legs at once like a flipper to drive himself backwards.

Once he reached the outcrop, he dragged himself ashore. The grey-and-green rock was surprisingly brittle, crumbling to gravel under his hands. Alex heaved Zoey up beside him, their hands clamming stickily together.

"That might be the single most disgusting thing that's ever happened to me." Zoey scooped clear goop off her cheeks and out of her fringe. Rock dust had stuck to her hand and she rubbed it between her fingers. "Dragon bogies. We're actually *inside* the dragon!"

She laughed – only a little manically – and Alex couldn't help but join in. They had made it! Their most ridiculous plan yet had actually worked. The most dangerous part might still lie ahead, but allowing himself this moment of triumph made it seem distinctly less impossible.

Plus it distracted him from the horror of being covered head-to-toe in dragon snot.

"Where's Anil?" he asked, sitting up so that slime sloughed off his skin.

Swinging movement overhead caught their attention. Anil hung upside down from a sticky green ribbon that had snagged his ankle. An air bubble sealed off his nose and mouth so they hadn't heard his calls for help.

"I'm stuck on mucus," Anil said as soon as the bubble was popped.

Their friend dangled too high above the snot rocks for them to reach. Alex moved to touch the mucus swamp, wondering if it would respond to his powers.

Zoey spoke before he could try. "Do you feel that? There's something..."

She lifted her head and glanced around, as if expecting to find something watching them. Alex stood up and brushed himself off. There seemed to be magic everywhere. Heavy on the air, glowing from every wall. It almost teased the magic out from inside him as if he had sprung a leak.

Zoey was right. A presence lurked behind it. The same intruding darkness he had felt sapping his connections to the infected animals.

"You can feel it too?" Alex asked.

Zoey nodded, flexing her fingers experimentally as if she had lost feeling there. Maybe being so close to the source of darkness meant you didn't need sea magic to sense it.

"I can feel it," Anil called. "Also, I can feel all my blood pooling inside my head."

"There's an easy way to get him down." Zoey picked up a craggy rock and let it fly. It hit Anil square in the chest and shattered into dust.

"Ow!" he cried.

"Just getting my eye in." Zoey chose another stone and threw. This time it sliced through the mucus string, sending Anil head first into the swamp with a dull splat.

Zoey dusted off her hands. "Not going to pretend I didn't enjoy that."

After hauling Anil from the gunk, they took a moment to get their bearings. Salty air rushed over their heads, the blowhole high above their heads flexing and tightening.

"This must connect all the way up to the dragon's lungs and nostrils," Anil said. "Its body must be so huge that after air gets all the way down here it needs another way out."

The airway walls quivered, wet and fleshy. Everywhere glowed dimly green, strings of mucus shining overhead like foul fairy lights. Slime was drying to a stiff crust on their skin.

"It smells like…" Zoey grimaced. "I actually can't think of anything as disgusting as the reality."

"We've smelled a lot of terrible things on our adventures, but this might be the worst," Anil agreed.

He reached eagerly into his pocket and removed a sodden clump of paper that had once been his notebook. Anil allowed himself a crestfallen moment, before perking up again to take a camera wrapped up in a waterproof case from his other pocket.

"There's absolutely nothing like this in the archive," he said, snapping pictures in all directions.

"Photos of mucus." Zoey shrugged her backpack off her shoulders. "Alert the media." She opened the bag to check their supplies were still in one piece. Kraken snoozed safely in her bag, the natural sedative keeping her oblivious to their journey.

The rest of the bag clinked and clanked with empty

vials and beakers. A larger bottle contained the pre-mixed cure recipe, awaiting a dose of zircongris to be complete.

"Meri asked me to take as many samples as I can," Zoey said, scraping some mucus into a vial. "Argosy probably wants some too."

Alex pressed a hand to his chest. The bottle of poison weighed heavily inside his pocket. He wouldn't actually use it – he had only taken it to keep Argosy onside. That's what he had told himself. But if they really couldn't cure the dragon...

Deeper in the backpack, he spotted a tangle of wires. They threaded through the sides of the bag into its front pouches. Alex reached for them but Zoey stopped him.

"I couldn't come here without a secret weapon up my sleeve," she said tantalizingly.

"You should probably just tell us what it is so we can use it to not die," Anil suggested.

Zoey wagged a finger. "That would be no fun."

The last piece of equipment in the backpack was a walkie-talkie. Alex flicked it on and brought it to his mouth.

"We've—"

"Don't forget your code name," Zoey demanded.

Alex sighed. "Invasive Invertebrate has landed."

A long moment of silence followed. They had accepted the risk that the thick walls of the dragon's body would block the signal. Alex had simply hoped for a little luck.

Just as he was about to give up, the walkie-talkie fuzzed.

"*Are Trembling Tapeworm and Doctor Dragon with you?*" came Meri's voice.

Zoey grinned. "And that's why I like her."

"We're all here." Alex spoke into the walkie-talkie. "Did everybody get away safely?"

"*We joined the* Dorothea *before sailing clear. The baby dragon protected us from the worst of the weather. It's getting so strong!*" said Meri. "*The storm wall opened to let us out. The dragon wanted us gone.*"

"Stay at a safe distance and watch the storm," Alex said. "If it begins to die away, that probably means the dragon is losing control to the parasites. Let us know right away."

"*We'll come and collect you once you've delivered the cure. If not...*" Meri trailed off. Nobody wanted to think about what would happen if they failed. "*We can regroup and plan our next move.*"

They had to act quickly to create and deliver the cure. If they didn't make it in time, any next move they could make was unlikely to be enough.

"Speak soon. Stay safe." Alex shut off the walkie-talkie. "Which way do we go?"

There was a pause before Anil realized they were looking to him for direction.

"Oh, you're going to follow me?"

"You've worked the hardest on learning about all this stuff," Alex said. "There's no one better to lead us."

Anil stood a little taller. "I'm just used to Zoey charging off so we have no choice but to follow."

"Maybe it's time we trusted somebody else then," Zoey said with a smile.

Anil peered up at the blowhole and spun around like a compass needle to get his bearings. "We want to go down the dragon's body. So it should be that way." He pointed his camera across the mucus swamp, where it lapped against the far wall.

"I really don't want to swim through that," Zoey said.

"Maybe we don't have to."

Anil climbed a spear of snot rock and reached for a thick string of mucus dangling from the roof. It held his weight, and he kicked his legs to swing back and forth. More mucus hung like vines, all the way across the clammy quagmire. Momentum carried Anil close enough to grab the next string.

"Come on!" he shouted, swinging towards the next hold.

"Is it bad that a small part of me was hoping he'd fall into the mucus again?" Zoey asked.

"Yes," replied Alex. "It *would* have been funny though."

Zoey went first, climbing the rock and swinging out

onto the mucus. Next, Alex grabbed the first vine. It squelched in his hand like wet rubber, grey water wringing from the tough slime. He swallowed down a shiver of revulsion and threw his weight forwards.

The mucus stretched but held firm. Alex quickly kicked his legs, already feeling the strain in his shoulder. He managed to swing enough that he could reach for the next vine with his free hand. The swamp blurred beneath him, momentum carrying him easily to the next string and the next.

"This is easier than I thou—"

A mucus string hit him in the face. He had caught up to Zoey too quickly and a vine she had just released had swung back into his path. Alex lost his grip and was knocked upside down. He prepared to give himself an air bubble as the swamp rushed up from below.

Something caught his ankle – Anil had loosed a lasso of mucus to wrap tightly around his foot. Dangling upside down, momentum swung him onwards. Zoey and Anil grabbed his hands and dragged him onto a dry bed of snot rock.

"Graceful," said Zoey, helping him to his feet.

Alex brushed himself off. "I try my best. Where now?"

Anil pointed to a dark opening in the wall, lit dimly green by the dragon's glow, hidden by a curtain of mucus and rimed with powdery snot. "It doesn't exactly look inviting."

"Let's get moving. We have a long way to go." Alex paused at the threshold of the opening. "Time to go into the belly of the beast."

"We're actually going into its bowel," Anil pointed out.

"I know. I was doing a dramatic last line before we plunge into danger."

"Oh, sorry!" Anil waved for him to carry on. "Do it again."

Alex took a deep breath. "Looks like it's time to...let's just go."

They parted the mucus curtain to begin their journey into the belly/bowel of the beast.

CHAPTER NINETEEN

THE BELLY OF THE BEAST

The soft pink pipe rippled and twitched as they crawled, denting under their hands and knees before plumping back up as they passed. Thick hairs bristled from odd angles, brittle crystals of dried mucus flaking away when disturbed. Heavy gusts of rancid air made them choke, sticky moisture beading on their skin.

"I always hoped saving the world would be more glamorous." Zoey wrung slime from her fringe and nudged Anil with her shoulder. "Maybe leave this part out of our story."

"This is hardship and personal sacrifice! It's important people know what we went through. Literally, in this case." Anil plucked a large crystal from a gristly hair. It cracked open and yellow gunk oozed over his hands. "All right, maybe I *won't* mention this bit."

A discordant creaking stopped them in their tracks. The internal soundscape of the dragon – mostly wet sucking noises and airy flatulence – made it impossible to tell where it came from.

"I really hope the dragon is just gassy," said Zoey.

Alex forced himself to keep moving. It was always going to feel unnatural to crawl around inside the Water Dragon. They couldn't allow themselves to be spooked by every peculiar sound. But another, stronger feeling was tiptoeing up Alex's spine. A sense of something *wrong*.

Corruption.

More than just the dimly glowing spongy walls of the pipe squeezed tight around him. The same force that stifled his connection to the dragon weighed heavily on his body here. The inside of the dragon had become its lair and they were crawling right into its grasp.

Still, nothing interrupted their journey towards the dragon's digestive system. The pipe continued a long way, viscous swill slurping at their elbows and curdled lumps of mucus clinging to their clothes. Eventually they reached a thick screen of hair.

"I think we can get through here," Zoey said.

The hair bent and flexed when she pushed, bristling

apart so she could squeeze through. Alex and Anil followed, tacky strands itching over their skin.

"It's like being tackled by a wet dog," Anil whined.

In the faint green light, Alex saw plastic bottles and shreds of fishing net tangled in the hairs. The barrier was obviously intended to prevent any foreign material getting deeper into the dragon's body.

"Litter must get in here when the dragon cleans up ocean rubbish," Alex said, scraping a syrupy crisp packet off his shoulder. The dragon sacrificed so much to try and protect the water, and this was how it was rewarded.

Once they were through the hair, a narrow space forced them to shuffle sideways for a while, before a wider passage opened up. Burbling groans and grating gurgles shook the walls and rumbled under their feet.

"I think we've just gone around the dragon's stomach," Zoey said.

Anil patted his belly. "I wouldn't say no to a snack."

They huddled on the spongy floor to eat sandwiches – safely wrapped in paper to stay mucus-free. Alex had already lost track of time. At least a few hours must have passed since they entered the dragon. It wasn't just the long journey that had left him weary. The constant, heavy strain of the corruptive force dragged at his limbs and throbbed inside his head.

"You okay?" Zoey leaned towards him. "I can still feel it – almost like an angry voice nagging in my mind. I just can't work out what it's saying."

Anil nodded, flexing his fingers experimentally. "It's almost a physical thing I want to force out of me."

Alex frowned. Before doing any of this, he should have considered what effect bringing his friends so close to the source of corruption would have on them. The sooner they were out of here, the better.

"Come on," he said, climbing to his feet. "It can't be much further now."

Another rending *creak* sounded from somewhere nearby. The walls rippled in response. Ahead, the faint green light flickered as if a shadow had passed across it. Alex watched for a long moment, but nothing else moved.

"I see something."

Zoey ran ahead before Alex could stop her. A short way further along the passage she slowed and began to take wide, exaggerated steps as if avoiding invisible obstacles.

"Great, now she's seeing things," said Anil.

"Look at my feet!" Zoey insisted.

She stepped again. The floor dimpled, like she was standing on the outside of an undercooked sausage, lightening from pink to pale. Alex and Anil stared at her blankly and Zoey huffed in frustration.

"I think this is like a sieve that only lets waste through to the bowel. It's keeping us out."

"I always knew I was nutritious," Anil said.

"We're walking too heavily!" Zoey slung off her backpack and laid it gently at her feet. After a moment, the passage quivered, and the bag sank through the floor.

"Kraken!" Alex cried.

"It's okay! I've got an idea." Zoey lowered herself down to lie flat on the soft floor, sprawling her arms and legs wide. "If we can spread our weight as much as possible, we should—"

The fibres of the floor seemed to loosen around her. Zoey sank too quickly for either of them to grab her, the floor swallowing her up before flexing back into place as if smacking its lips.

CHAPTER TWENTY

FINALLY, SOMETHING MAGICAL

"Zoey!"

They scrabbled at the floor but it refused to yield.

Anil straightened up and inhaled an exaggerated deep breath. "Okay, she said we have to relax."

"I can't relax when one of my best friends just got swallowed by dragon guts!"

Gently, Anil took Alex's arm and guided him to the floor. They lay down, side by side, and splayed their limbs, trying to spread their weight as widely as possible. Alex held his breath, heart thundering in his chest, waiting for the ground to open up.

Nothing happened.

"You're too tense!" Anil scolded. "Focus on your magic."

"What do you mean?"

"Think about how it feels when you first call on your power. The rush of salt water running through your veins." Anil softened his voice. "It feels good, right?"

Alex took a longer breath and felt his heartbeat begin to slow. "It makes me feel safe. And proud. Because it's been entrusted to me."

"It makes you part of a centuries-long story," Anil said. "All that history and power, tingling on your fingertips like nibbling fish."

"Exactly. How do you know what it feels—?"

Before he could lift his head and finish the question, the floor seemed to melt underneath them. They sank quickly, flesh closing over them and undulating rhythmically to funnel them along.

Light flared, and Alex fell into empty space as the floor – apparently now the ceiling – spat him out. He landed at Zoey's feet just as she was wringing putrid water from her sleeve to splatter on his face.

"That was honestly an accident," she said.

Zoey helped him up. There was enough space to stand straight. Pink ridged walls peeled away ahead of them like a cave. Below, a dark basin of water glowed bright with colour: blossoming greens and frills of yellow, branching pinks and opulent blues. Shadows of fish drifted sluggishly below the surface.

"It's a coral reef," Alex said.

Zoey smiled wearily. "Finally, something magical instead of disgusting."

Anil grabbed his camera to begin snapping photos.

The softly ridged walls offered supple holds for them to climb down to a lower level. In places, the top of the reef broke the water, providing safe islands for them to stand.

"This isn't how I imagined the inside of a bowel," Alex said. "Is this where we'll find zircongris?"

Anil crouched beside the water. "This seems right to me. It might be in the reef."

Zoey leaned down beside him, brow furrowing. "I think there's something wrong with the fish."

Fat silver bodies lingered aimlessly around the reef, lazy tail flicks wafting the fish along. Alex looked closer. Their shape was unusual. Streamlined scales broke into a deep hollow halfway along their backs.

Alex frowned. "Are those...?"

Bite marks. Every fish was missing a crescent-shaped chunk from its back. Shreds of skin and scales trailed from the wounds.

"Zombie fish," whispered Zoey.

"But what took a bite out of them in the first place?" Anil asked.

They scanned the water but saw no sign of anything else moving. No predator alarmed the placid fish.

"If the zircongris might be here, we have to search. We dive quickly and stick together," Alex said, looking between his friends. "If we see anything suspicious, we come back to high ground."

Zoey took off her backpack and emptied it. Kraken stirred in her bag. If they found zircongris in the reef, it wouldn't be long before she was cured.

"Why don't you just leave the whole thing?" Alex asked as Zoey shouldered the empty backpack.

"Trust me," she said. "We might need it."

The water was cold enough to make them gasp as they stepped off their island and it lapped around their waists. At least it was considerably less sticky than what they had faced so far. Alex briefly flared his magic to open air bubbles around their mouths. Then they exchanged silent nods and ducked beneath the surface.

The lights and colours of the reef were quickly blotted by darkness below their feet, making it impossible to tell the depth of the water. Alex led the way, kicking his feet gently so Zoey and Anil could easily follow his path.

The zombie fish were definitely alive. Although they moved sluggishly, keen eyes flickered to watch the passing swimmers. Some were missing multiple small chunks of flesh while others had whole spines exposed to the water.

Zoey tapped his side and pointed through the murky water. Green light glowed from a little deeper, but that was hardly unusual. She pointed harder and grabbed his hand to make him descend. The glow grew brighter, casting a halo through the water.

The light was coming from the coral itself. Clefts and crevasses in the shelves of rock blazed as if seafire burned within them.

Alex kicked closer and peered into the coral. Soft lumps of green, clay-like material grew in bulbs from the rock. It matched the illustration Argosy had shown them. Alex was sure its light grew brighter as he moved closer.

After peeking inside another crack, Zoey whirled to face him. She mouthed a single word.

Zircongris!

The gap was just wide enough for Alex to squeeze his arm inside. Before he could get past his wrist, Anil grabbed his shoulder and pointed frantically above them. Alex shrugged him off – the zircongris was so close! – but Anil refused to be ignored.

Annoyed, Alex glanced up. He expected to be shown a tarnished piece of treasure or some disgusting biological detail to be photographed.

Instead, he felt his blood turn to ice.

A large creature detached itself from the nearby coral. Its wide, flat body was covered by plates of clear armour. Alex could see straight through it as six thick legs kicked to drive the creature powerfully through the water. Eyes like blank stones searched the darkness. Slowly, a set of mandibles slid from its face, serrated jaws snagged with scales and skin.

Alex had seen one of these monsters before. Then, it had only been visible through a microscope.

Now the parasite was *huge*.

CHAPTER TWENTY-ONE

BACK FROM THE DEAD (AGAIN)

The parasite's transparent body contorted the lights of the reef, twisting them into a corona of collapsing colours through its shell. A single, powerful stroke of its armoured legs brought it surging towards Alex.

He kicked himself away from the coral, floundering backwards. There was no way he would be fast enough to escape, but he might be able to block it from reaching his friends.

The monster's razor mandibles cranked open. Alex braced himself to feel its bite.

Blinding green light erupted around him. It blazed through the water, cleaving through the gloom. The parasite screeched, eyes and jaw twitching, before it veered away to shelter in the crevasse of a nearby rock.

Two sets of hands seized Alex's shoulders and hauled him away. The light seemed to radiate from Zoey, too bright to look at directly. Instead, he focused on Anil and followed him to the surface.

The air bubbles around their mouths popped as they scrambled onto a dry reef top. Alex fell panting onto his back and peered up at Zoey. The green light shone around her head and shoulders like a halo.

"How are you doing that?"

She grinned and pressed a button on the strap of her backpack. The light flickered and dimmed. Zoey shrugged off the bag and held it up to show them.

Thick glass tubes had been fed through slits in the fabric, looping back inside the bag so they lay flat against its exterior, hidden by a flap. Embers of green light faded inside the tubes.

"I thought there was a good chance we'd encounter more infected animals, so I filled some old camping lanterns with seafire and sewed them into my backpack. It works like the tanning-bed door did back on *The Dragonfly*." Zoey slung it back over her shoulders. "I didn't expect we'd have to use it against parasites the size of badgers."

"Bigger! More like sheep or one of those small horses."

Anil scanned the water for any sign of parasite pursuit. "Are they supposed to get that big?"

"Maybe the bigger the host, the bigger the parasites grow inside it. And the dragon is *really* big."

Alex shivered inside his wet clothes as he got to his feet. "If they're that big, the dragon won't be able to hold them off much longer. We have to go back down there and get the zircongris. There's no other way."

Both Zoey and Anil regarded the water sceptically. Now they knew what had taken bites out of the fish, it was too easy to imagine bites being taken out of them. But neither of his friends argued. A shard of guilt jabbed Alex in the gut. They would face any danger he asked of them.

"How much do we need?" asked Anil.

"A couple of bulbs." Zoey pressed the button and the backpack light flared again. "The light should keep the parasite away. Stay close to me."

Alex and Anil huddled either side of her and they plunged back into the water together. The backpack shrouded them in a protective force field of green light. As they descended, zombie fish twisted away in ragged shoals to avoid the glow.

The mangled bodies of the infected fish made it difficult to watch for the giant parasite. Only when the shoals had cleared did they spot the monster, lurking in the safety of the shadows, flicking its legs lazily to follow them.

Alex lifted an arm and focused his magic. He *pushed* through the water, aiming a sharp current to knock the monster away.

The parasite simply drifted back into place, blank eyes fixed, mandibles twitching as if in anticipation of the first bite.

Below them, the glowing coral rose into view. Zoey turned her back so the light would shield them and Anil served as lookout, allowing Alex to reach into the smouldering crevasse.

The soft bulbs of zircongris shone brighter as Alex stretched his fingertips towards them. Even leaning his whole weight forwards, shoulder grinding against the rugged coral, the precious material remained tantalizingly out of reach.

Briefly, he looked beyond the guardian light. The parasite was poised nearby, patiently waiting for any opening it could exploit. Alex had already seen how quickly the monster could move – one mistake and it would make them pay.

He shifted his weight and reached again. It was *just* too far!

A tap on his shoulder made him turn. Anil offered his pen. Alex was briefly confused – you can't write underwater! – until Anil made a scooping motion and he understood.

The pen gave him the extra reach he needed. He fumbled its tip against the soft clay of the zircongris, before swiping the pen like a knife. The material broke free of the rock and Alex quickly speared it.

Behind him, Zoey was waiting to grab it. The zircongris flared bright when it touched her hand before dimming as she dropped the lump into a clear plastic bag.

Movement elsewhere on the reef snatched Alex's attention. He jerked back instinctively, colliding painfully with the coral.

More parasites emerged from the shadows. A pack of them pushed towards the light before recoiling from its glare. Instead of attacking head on, the monsters spread out to surround them, pinning the group against the reef.

Zoey jabbed a finger towards the crevasse and Alex whirled around to reach inside again. The next bulb of zircongris was too far away, even with the added reach of the pen.

There was no time to mess around. Alex splayed his fingers. This time he *pulled* on the water as if trying to draw it into his body. A draught of water swished through the crevasse, strong enough to break the zircongris free and send it skipping towards him.

Alex tried to catch the bulb but it bobbled over his hands and tumbled away from the coral.

Directly towards the parasites.

Anil kicked recklessly to send himself lunging after the zircongris. He snatched it at full stretch before it could sail into darkness, the material blazing bright in his grip.

The daring manoeuvre had pushed him to the edge of the light. Parasites surged towards him, mandibles gnashing.

Alex and Zoey grabbed Anil's feet and hauled him back into the light. The parasites arced away at the last moment, jaws snipping empty water.

Huddled together once again, the group pushed away from the reef. Now all they needed to do was escape the water, retrieve their equipment, and find somewhere safe to complete the cure.

The dazzling green light of the backpack held strong, but the parasites saw their opportunity slipping away and decided to test their luck. Taking turns, they brushed the edge of the force field, shuddering away from its touch before wheeling around to try again. Alex sent out currents of water to try and hold them off, but the parasites harried from all sides.

Finally, Alex pointed both hands downwards and *pushed* as hard as he could. A current drove them rapidly upwards, pressure popping in his ears. It caught the parasites by surprise, leaving them scrambling to follow.

As soon as they broke the surface, gasping with fear rather than lack of air, they ran for their stash of equipment. Zoey loaded it quickly into the glowing backpack, along with the clear bag of precious zircongris.

"Maybe they can't follow us out of the water?" Anil panted.

A parasite burst from the water and scrabbled up onto the top of the reef, sharp legs breaking off pieces of rock.

Anil sighed. "Never mind, time to run."

Together they skipped across the reef top. The parasites were slower on land but no less terrifying. Their deadly jaws hissed and creaked. The backpack light was weaker out of the water, the range of its shield reduced to a tiny island.

At the edge of the reef, Alex, Anil and Zoey leaped across onto pillowy flesh.

"Don't stop," Alex panted, pushing his friends ahead of him.

A squeal from above made him ignore his own command. He looked up to see a parasite drop from the ceiling. It hit Alex hard, sharp legs cinching tight as they rolled across the soft ground.

Out of range of the light.

Alex came to a stop on his back, the weight of the parasite pressing him into the spongy ground. He brought his hands up to push the monster's head away before its mandibles could cut into his throat. Alex held it there as the razor jaws scissored open and closed, seeking his flesh.

More parasites saw the opportunity and swarmed towards him.

"Go!" he shouted, hoping his friends would see it was hopeless and leave him to complete their task. Nothing was more important than making the cure, saving Kraken and then the Water Dragon.

A battle cry tore through the air. Something collided with the parasite on top of him and knocked it away. Zoey and Anil were still out of reach, watching on in horror. Another figure, tall and broad, stood over him. They wore a tattered raincoat, heavy hood pulled low to conceal their face, and wildly swung an oar to smash the other parasites away.

"Come on," they said gruffly, extending a calloused hand.

Alex took it and was hauled roughly to his feet. Zoey and Anil hurried back to bring them under the protection of the light.

"I couldn't get to you," Zoey said, face pale with fear.

"Do you know a way out?" Alex asked the stranger. There was no time to ask who they were or what they were doing here. Trust, no matter how temporary, was their only chance of escape.

The stranger turned to the wall and stroked one of its ridges. The wall twitched as if ticklish and some kind of valve shuddered open, a circle of pink flesh with a puckering split in the middle. Wide enough for them to fit inside.

"Where does it go?" Alex asked.

"No time!" Zoey threw herself head first into the valve.

Behind them, the parasites were regrouping. Zoey's kicking legs were swallowed up and Anil climbed after her, the valve closing around his middle to guzzle him down.

"This is your only choice," the hooded figure said.

Alex nodded and jumped inside. The tube was smaller now, forcing him to wriggle through. The stranger shoved him by the feet and squeezed in behind.

The valve closed up, leaving the snapping parasites on the other side. The walls undulated, massaging Alex along, the stranger bumping against his ankles.

Eventually, the pipe spat them into a shallow pool of greasy water. Zoey and Anil splashed over to help Alex up, leaving the stranger to bring themselves to their feet.

Their coat had fallen off one shoulder and the hood peeled away from their face.

Alex gasped. "It's impossible."

Raze Callis stood before them, once again raised from the dead.

CHAPTER TWENTY-TWO

NOT-SO-SMALL INTESTINE

A series of arched chambers flexed walls of dark muscle, squeezing tight over their heads. Thick strands of seaweed trailed from above and tangled around their ankles in shallow water, soaking up the faint light so they stood in murky, swaying shadow.

Alex wanted to grab his friends and run. Seeing Callis here was like meeting a ghoul, a danger they had long ceased to fear and were no longer prepared to face. Doubt gnawed at his stomach and his knees shook. It simply shouldn't have been *possible.*

Callis smirked. "I know what you're thinking."

"You smell like a fishmonger's apron," Zoey said.

"All right, perhaps I didn't know after all."

Alex took a deep breath of foul air and stood as tall as he could. "You're supposed to be dead."

"*That's* what I knew you'd be thinking." Callis chuckled deep in his throat. It sounded wet, as if seawater wallowed in his lungs. "Lucky for me, the Water Dragon doesn't chew its food."

Alex had not seen Raze Callis, poacher and pirate, since he had disappeared down the throat of the Water Dragon after trying to steal its only egg. Before that, he had been presumed lost after a fierce storm summoned by the dragon to evade capture.

This duo of improbable survivals had clearly taken a toll. Although Callis's frame remained tall and broad, his sun-starved skin now clung tightly to his bones. A hunch bowed him crookedly forwards as if he suffered perpetual seasickness. His hair had grown grey and his thin sideburns had become scraggly whiskers.

"There are not many advantages to being trapped inside a dragon, but I thought I'd at least got away from you three." Callis sighed. "I assume you're not here to rescue me?"

"No, we're here to—" Anil began.

Zoey punched him to stay quiet. But there was no time to keep the mission secret. Dropping to her knees, she riffled through the contents of her backpack. First she brought out the precious zircongris, then a stoppered bottle brimming with dull grey liquid, followed by empty test tubes and a narrow-brimmed flask.

Lastly, she carefully lifted out Kraken. The octopus stirred inside her bag, eyes swivelling hazily and skin still blazing red as she revived from her slumber.

Anil stepped in front of Zoey to serve as a guard in case Callis tried to interfere. Their old nemesis simply watched on curiously.

"What's wrong with your cephalopod friend?"

Anger spilled over inside Alex. "As if you don't know!"

Callis blinked. "For once I have no need to feign innocence."

"The parasites!" Alex stepped up to him. "You expect me to believe you're not responsible?"

"You think...?" Callis tossed back his head and laughed, throwing his arms wide. "I've been living inside a small intestine. My free time has been occupied exclusively by survival. The parasites, you may have noticed, make that a particularly difficult task."

Zoey used tweezers to break free a fragment of zircongris and drop it into a flask filled with clear water. She swirled it around and the material dissolved, flushing the water light green.

Creating the cure was clearly going to take some time. Callis might try and interfere at any moment. The best thing Alex could do was keep his nemesis talking. The pirate rarely needed much encouragement.

"Tell me how you stayed alive."

"When I splashed down into the dragon's stomach, I knew I had only minutes to avoid being digested," Callis began. "Fortunately, plenty of debris was swallowed alongside me – your precious dragon really isn't a picky eater. I rode a broken piece of my ship to safety. After that, as you've no doubt discovered, a creature this size contains plenty of air bubbles and unusual crannies to help me survive."

Zoey shoved the flask of diluted zircongris into Anil's hands while she grabbed a pipette and test tube. Carefully, she drew up and measured out a small dose of the green solution.

"It's been ages since you were swallowed," Alex said. "Why didn't you escape?"

Callis dropped his mouth open and slapped a grubby hand against his jaw. "Now why didn't I think of that? Instead of an endless, terrifying fight for my life within the viscera of a giant monster, I could simply have waltzed to freedom. Silly me!"

"Being trapped in here has made him really sarcastic," Anil noted.

Zoey nodded appreciatively. "I kind of like it."

"Some ways are impassable." The pirate's face turned grim as he continued. "The parasites appeared shortly after my arrival. They make things even more difficult. They're extremely aggressive creatures. I had no choice but to hide from them. This small intestine is a particular favourite of mine."

Alex glanced around the pulsing muscle walls. There was no obvious way out. Callis had trapped them there.

"The parasites have been infecting sea animals," Anil explained. "We thought it was bad enough dealing with little ones."

"You've seen nothing yet," Callis intoned darkly. "The parasites here grow in number the higher you travel up the dragon's body."

Only a few of the armoured monsters had already seemed like too many to handle. It was unnerving to see genuine fear in Callis's eyes. He wasn't trying to scare them; everything he said was simply the truth of what they faced.

"You saved me," Alex said. He looked at his hands, one still bandaged from the electrocution, the other covered in cuts and grazes from holding the parasite at bay.

Callis scoffed. "Believe me when I say I would gladly have watched you all be chewed to mincemeat. But I haven't quite given up on getting out of this place. With your powers and the girl's equipment—"

"I have a name," Zoey interjected without looking up from her work.

"And I'm useful too," Anil added.

"—I figure we might just stand a chance."

Finally, Zoey picked up the bottle of unfinished cure and removed the stopper. A small amount of liquid zircongris had been measured into a test tube. Now she added it to the grey mixture and stirred it with a metal stick. The dull solution instantly sparkled green, growing brighter as it blended together.

Hope soared in Alex's heart. He pointed to Kraken. "Quick!"

Anil picked up the octopus's bag while Zoey measured a dose of the cure into a pipette. As soon as Anil opened a corner of the bag, Kraken snaked an arm through to try and tear it wider. Zoey quickly squirted the cure inside.

The seawater fizzed. Kraken abandoned her escape attempt, a shudder making her drop back to the bottom.

Alex reached for the bag. "It's hurting her."

Zoey caught his wrist. "Just wait."

The convulsions intensified; Kraken's arms curled tight to her body. Finally, she stilled. Her arms unfurled and the angry red drained from her skin. Splotches of green took its place, mirroring the gleam of the antidote, spreading rapidly until it covered her entire body. Her eyes focused and she reached up to push insistently at the top of the bag.

"Let her out!" Alex said.

Kraken leaped into his arms, wrapping her suckers snugly around his neck and nuzzling his face hard enough to smother him.

"It worked." Alex held her tight. A lump in his throat, as well as Kraken's tight grip, threatened to choke off his words. "You're back."

"This is all very touching, but—" Callis began to say.

Kraken lifted her head, arched her body, and spat a bullet of water at the pirate. It dashed hard against his face.

"I thought she was cured!" he spluttered.

"She's not infected any more," Zoey said. "She just hates you."

The cure worked. The zircongris really had been the last piece of the puzzle. The giant parasites were a problem but they could still save the Water Dragon. They just needed to reach the source of infection.

"You're a genius!" Alex crowed, pulling Zoey into a hug before reaching for Anil too. "You both are!"

Zoey beamed. "Well, duh."

"Teamwork makes the dream work," said Anil.

Callis laughed, hard enough to double himself over and lean on his knees for support. Alex broke free of his friends.

"What's so funny?"

"I should have known." The pirate straightened up and dabbed at his eyes. "Of *course* you would try and save the dragon. You can't resist doing the 'right thing', even when it's clearly idiotic."

Alex would have preferred to keep their plan secret, but Callis had seen enough to guess it.

The amusement dropped from the pirate's face. "Will your cure work?"

Zoey lifted her chin. "You've just seen for yourself."

"I can help." A hint of desperation had come into Callis's voice. "There are ways to move through the dragon that the parasites don't use. I can help you travel safely."

Alex glared. "It wasn't long ago you tried to kill the dragon."

"And now I simply wish to escape it. I'll help you, if you promise to take me with you after the dragon is cured."

Zoey vehemently shook her head. "There's no way we can trust him." She looked to Anil for support, but he was peering thoughtfully around the small intestine.

"We don't know how to reach the dragon's brain. I can't even see a way out of here," he said. "If Callis can show us the way, it's the best chance we have of getting there in time to save the dragon. And at least if he's with us we can keep an eye on him, instead of always watching our backs."

"So that's what you bring to the group." Callis wagged a finger at him. "Common sense."

Zoey screwed up her face. "Never thought I'd hear that."

Trusting Callis went against every natural instinct in Alex's body. But there was nothing natural about any of this. Maybe the only way to battle the bizarre was to embrace it.

Callis offered help only to save himself. That, at least, Alex could trust.

"All right," he said. "We'll go together."

"Excellent!" Callis clapped his hands. "That means I can show you the way out of this small intestine. I suggest you follow me."

CHAPTER TWENTY-THREE

BROWN PENCIL REQUIRED

The squishy terrain of the Water Dragon's small intestine proved no challenge for Callis, his time-worn boots easily avoiding deeper puddles and tangles of seaweed, his large frame shifting deftly to keep his balance. No wonder he had managed to survive for so long.

"Not like that." Callis snatched the pencil from Anil's grip and slashed a hard line across the damp page of his notebook. It had dried just enough for him to begin mapping the territory. "It's steep, like this."

Alex and Zoey trailed close behind, making sure their footsteps matched the safe path picked out by the pirate.

"Doctor Dragon to *The Dragonfly*," Zoey said into the walkie-talkie. "Do you copy?"

No reply came through the speaker.

"If you can hear this, we've acquired some zircongris and made the cure! Now we're heading up the dragon to reach its brain."

She glanced at Alex, silently asking if she should mention their new companion. He shook his head and Zoey shut off the walkie-talkie.

"Do you really think we can trust him?" Zoey asked.

Kraken grabbed Alex's chin and jerked his head roughly from side to side.

"I know!" Alex narrowed his eyes at Callis ahead. "But I trust that he wants to save himself. Right now, we're the best way for him to do that."

"What happens when we're not the best option any more?"

"We'll worry about that later."

"Ah, our classic planning method!" Zoey lowered her voice again. "We shouldn't help him escape. Not after everything he's done."

"That was my first reaction too." A cold shard in Alex's heart made him want to abandon Callis here and condemn him to whichever bitter end found him first. It would be what he deserved. "But that's not who we are. We have to be better than him."

Kraken gripped his neck a little tighter to make it clear she didn't agree.

Callis glanced over his shoulder. "Plotting against me already?"

Beside him, Alex felt Zoey bristle like a sea urchin. "Just tell us where we're going."

"We head to the higher plateau of the small intestine." He wrinkled his nose. "It's so disgusting that even parasites don't go there."

Anil squeaked delightedly and plucked a brown colouring pencil from inside his jacket.

"That leads us into the stomach. From there, we'll pass the lungs and heart to reach the dragon's brain. Well, that's the theory."

Alex arched an eyebrow. "Why is it only a theory?"

"I've never made it beyond the stomach," Callis admitted. "There's a heavy concentration of parasites there and...other hazards. But your magic light may be enough to get us through."

Ahead, the muscle walls curved abruptly upwards, forming a straight, circular shaft above their heads. Thick, white ridges like ribs circled the pipe at regular intervals. A waterfall of red liquid poured down the shaft, splashing the walls and spattering their clothes.

Anil paled. "Is that...?"

"Probably best not to think about it." Zoey wiped a red droplet from her cheek and shivered.

"Some of us are used to a little blood." Callis cracked his knuckles, a series of sharp pops like gunshots. "Time to climb."

The pipe was sheer enough that scaling it seemed impossible. Callis saw their doubt and reached for the first rung of cartilage. The white ring flexed under his grip, stretching the fleshy wall of the shaft, but held firm as he pulled himself up. The blood waterfall gushed down the centre of the pipe, leaving enough space around the edges that the pirate remained mostly dry.

"Come on." Callis reached down a calloused hand.

The three friends exchanged identical uncertain looks. It would be so easy for the pirate to throw them down.

Alex took a deep breath, nearly choking on the coppery air, and stepped up. There was no reason for Callis to betray them now. They had decided to trust their old enemy – if only temporarily – and it was up to Alex to prove it wasn't the worst idea he had ever had.

He really hoped he wouldn't be proved wrong.

The first rung was too high for Alex to reach by himself. So he gripped Callis's hand and let the pirate heave him up. Apparently being trapped inside the dragon hadn't diminished his strength.

"You can thank me later." Callis smirked.

"Don't push your luck."

Zoey was pulled up next, leaving Anil at the bottom

of the shaft. The narrow platform of cartilage wasn't big enough to hold them all.

"You could go up to the next one and leave space for—" Callis began.

"I don't want us to split up," Alex interrupted. "Anyway, it'll take too long. There must be a better way."

Zoey peered thoughtfully at the seaweed that trailed along the walls of the shaft. "Maybe we can rig up some kind of rope and pulley system."

"If only somebody here had magical sea powers," Anil called from below. "Remember when you made seaweed do your bidding before?"

Alex felt like an idiot for not thinking of it. Gently, he pressed a hand against the slick wall of the shaft. A *push* sent magic flowing from his fingertips. Power spread along the shaft and reached the seaweed. Slimy tendrils twitched, curling and fluttering as if waking from a deep sleep. Slowly, seaweed strands snaked towards them. They wrapped snugly around Anil's waist and hoisted him off the ground, whisking him up and above the others.

"I remember this trick," Callis said, as seaweed squirmed under his armpits. "I didn't much like it last time."

Alex smothered a smile. It probably didn't hurt to remind his old nemesis what might happen to him if betrayal crossed his mind.

More seaweed crept down to pick up Alex and Zoey. Its cold clamminess made him shiver as tough strands formed a belt around his waist. Kraken held on tight as Alex was plucked off the cartilage and hoisted up, the blood waterfall thundering past them.

The seaweed deposited them on a higher ridge as more vines descended to scoop them up and continue the ascent. Magic flowed easily from Alex now, connecting him with the seaweed strands as if they were extensions of his own limbs. It made him feel jubilant, as if he were single-handedly beating back the dark power of the parasites.

A rumble somewhere above made the shaft tremble. The flow of the waterfall briefly slackened.

"What was that?" Anil shouted. He had been carried the highest, Alex and Callis directly below, Zoey after them.

"Maybe we should hurry," she shouted.

"Don't worry!" Alex called back.

He squeezed a fist and the seaweed holding Callis abruptly dropped. The pirate cried out as he was swung down and around in a streaking arc. Alex opened his hand at the top and the seaweed let Callis go.

"No!" the pirate bellowed as he flew towards the blood falls.

Another strand of seaweed snatched him from the air

at the last moment. Alex laughed, relishing the mastery of his magic, and extended a hand towards Zoey.

She glared daggers at him. "Don't you d—"

Too late. Her seaweed harness whipped her upwards like a fairground ride. Anil's released him at the same time and the animated strands swapped over, juggling the pair acrobatically between them.

"Extremely not okay with this!" Zoey shouted.

Anil's face flashed past. "This is fun but also I'm going to vomit!"

Alex laughed. The intensity of his magic somehow made him feel more connected to his friends, almost as if he could use his power to reach out to them like he could with animals. Being inside the Water Dragon seemed to heighten everything.

Above them all, a wider shelf of cartilage came into view at the top of the shaft. A passage extended beyond it.

"If you're quite finished trying to kill us, that's our way out," Callis said.

The seaweed deposited Anil onto the shelf first, setting him onto wobbly legs. Callis was dropped next – a little harder than strictly necessary – closely followed by Alex with Kraken on his shoulder.

Another rumble, harder than before, shuddered the length of the shaft. The flow of the waterfall pulsated, splashing blood against the walls. The ribs of cartilage squeezed, shaking loose the anchored strands of seaweed. Alex focused his magic to try and hold it up, but the vines were already shearing away, leaving Zoey dangling precariously.

Desperately, Alex flung his arm sideways. The seaweed followed, slamming Zoey into the wall of the shaft. She scrabbled for grip and managed to grab onto a lower ridge as the seaweed tumbled away, leaving her hanging by her fingertips.

"The parasites know we're coming," Alex said. "They're using the dragon's body against us."

Anil was already searching for a way down, but the drop from the shelf was too big. Callis shoved them both aside and rolled up his sleeves.

"Be ready to pull us back up."

He slung his legs over the edge of the shelf and squirmed down until his feet found the lower ridge. The shaft quaked again, almost knocking him off balance. Callis dropped to his knees and extended a hand to Zoey.

She hesitated, even now struggling to trust, glancing around for another way out. When no alternative plan presented itself, Zoey took one hand off the ridge to seize Callis's outstretched hand.

Time briefly stood still. Callis could simply flick his wrist and send Zoey tumbling to her doom. All at once it seemed senseless to have trusted him. Alex dropped to his knees to climb down, hoping it wasn't too late.

Then Callis was hauling Zoey up onto the ridge. They huddled together as the shaft quaked harder, threatening to hurl them over the precipice.

Alex pressed his hand flat to the ground and reached for the dragon. *Please*, he begged. *Stop this.*

The plea was cut short by the sapping force of the parasites. The dragon wouldn't hear him, couldn't stop Zoey and Callis from being shaken loose to tumble down the shaft.

Anil's hand landed on his shoulder. At the same time, magic spilled out of him in a torrent. The force of it broke the dam and his cry surged along his connection with the dragon.

"Please!"

The rumbling dampened and the waterfall slowed to a trickle. Quickly, Alex and Anil reached down to drag Zoey and Callis up onto the higher plateau of the small intestine. Together, they turned away from the shaft and fled into the connecting passage as the rumbling began to intensify again.

"Have I proved you can trust me now?" Callis asked as they ran.

"For now," Alex shouted back.

There were so many weird things going on that his old nemesis was beginning to become the least of his worries.

CHAPTER TWENTY-FOUR

MANY BAD SMELLS

They had encountered a lot of terrible smells on their recent adventures, but the Water Dragon's stomach was easily the worst.

"It smells like—" Zoey began, before her face turned green and a nauseated heave choked off her words.

Anil's voice was muffled by both hands covering his nose and mouth. "Can a smell kill you? I think it's eating my skin."

Only Callis appeared unruffled by the stink, so Alex did his best to pretend it didn't bother him either. Unfortunately that required him to breathe through his mouth. The swampy air tasted distinctly of rotten fish.

The stomach was the largest bodily cavern they had

encountered yet. Marbled red walls soared overhead, running with pink mucus. Phosphorescent algae glowed green in wavering curves and slashes to mark volatile tidelines. Most of the space was drowned under grey, watery fluid. Stalagmites of white salt crystals speared from the water like twisted sculptures.

"We can swim through," Anil said, moving towards the fluid.

Callis barred his way with an arm. Then he scooped up a tin can that had washed ashore and threw it into the swamp. The fluid fizzed and bubbled violently, dissolving the metal within seconds.

"Okay, swimming *might* be a bad idea," Anil accepted.

"Stomach acid," said Zoey.

Anil nodded. "It's not usually strong enough to burn right away."

"It's not usually inside a magic dragon," Alex replied.

Some items had survived the stomach acid. In the middle of the swamp, an island of salt rose high above the waterline. It was a graveyard of maritime gear: crumpled buoys were littered like punctured beach balls and a vast length of fishing net was spiked on the tip of a salt spire. The splintered bow of an old ship lay on its side, wood blackened with rot.

"There's so much litter in the ocean that animals eat it

by mistake," Alex said. "Maybe the Water Dragon is no different."

"Eating me was no accident," grumbled Callis.

Zoey sneered. "You're enough to make anybody sick."

Nothing stirred in the swamp or moved on the island of salt. A purring gurgle vibrated lightly through the walls, flesh quivering with a hungry groan.

"No sign of parasites," Alex noted.

Callis scanned around. "They'll be here. We have to find a way across. When the dragon eats, some debris gets thrown clear of the acid. That's how I survived. And I think I've spotted something that could help us."

He led the way around the edge of the swamp, picking a path through crusty seaweed and mummified fish, a sheared shard of a ship's anchor and crushed lobster pots. After a few minutes, they reached a wooden rowing boat, washed up just clear of the acid tide.

"This might get us across," Callis said.

Zoey shook her head. "The acid will dissolve it in seconds flat."

"Is there a way we can protect it?"

Alex scratched at a salt stalagmite and rubbed the coarse crystals between his fingers. Kraken copied the motion. The salt seemed to withstand the worst of the corrosive acid. Maybe there was a way to use that to their advantage.

Carefully, he kneeled and pressed a hand to the ground. It was wet but didn't burn his skin. Alex let his magic leak out and spread into the water. Around them, the algae glowed brighter as if recognizing his power.

There was enough seawater in the dragon's stomach that he could draw the salt from it. The water turned white, as if crusting over. Crystals and flakes of salt feathered the surface. Alex flicked a finger and it flowed towards the rowing boat on a current, lifting up to creep across the wood.

"Maybe you could coat us too?" suggested Anil. "Just in case."

Callis scoffed. "You'd just be seasoning the parasites' next meal."

The salty water spread across the rowing boat, fanning over the wood as it hardened, crackling to a stiff crust until the whole craft – including the oars – was encased in a thick layer of salt.

"Quickly," said Callis, already pushing the boat into the swamp. Everybody hopped inside.

"If we see the parasites—" Alex began.

"*When* we see the parasites," Callis interrupted. "We stay quiet for as long as we can and hope they don't notice us. When they do, we use the light to keep them away for long enough to…"

"Uh oh," Zoey said. "He's started trailing off suspiciously."

"I've never managed to escape before!" Callis snapped. "I don't want to jinx it."

"We do jinx things quite a lot," Anil acknowledged.

It felt wrong to let Callis take the lead. Usually their plans were designed to achieve the exact opposite of whatever he wanted. But they had brought him along for his experience of navigating inside the dragon. So Alex took a seat in the boat as Callis launched it onto the swamp and took up the oars.

The salt made the rowing boat heavy and it dipped low in the water, the acid rising worryingly close along the sides. Salt sizzled and popped in the corrosive fluid, a trail of white dissolving behind them. Kraken shifted to sit on top of Alex's head, as far away from the acid as possible.

There was still no sign of skittering legs or gnashing mandibles. The walls appeared empty, the algae lighting a path below a dark roof.

Alex leaned towards his friends, speaking quietly enough that he hoped Callis wouldn't hear over the swish of the oars in the water.

"Something happened back there," he said. "When you were in trouble, Zoey. Did you feel anything?"

Zoey's brow crinkled. "I felt the dragon's power. Stronger than I've ever felt it before. Like it was reaching out directly to help me."

"It was like..." Anil paused to think. "Almost like I was you."

"What do you mean?" Alex asked.

Anil flexed his fingertips, studying them closely, before he shook his head. "Never mind. It's stupid."

During the rescue, Alex was sure he had felt connected to his friends, almost as if threads of sea magic knitted them together. He had only found the strength to break through to the Water Dragon when Anil joined him. It had felt, Alex realized now, just like when he had fought alongside the baby dragon. Another source of power intertwining with his own.

But that would mean...

"Watch out!" Callis called.

Nearby, the syrupy surface of the swamp bulged into a fat bubble. When it burst, the blistering stench of rotten eggs bombarded the boat.

"It'll take more than a bad smell to stop us," Alex said, ignoring the brief flash of dizziness it inflicted on him. Kraken turned yellow and squirmed inside his T-shirt.

Zoey laughed. "I thought that would be much worse."

The water erupted in a rushing plume, spraying directly upwards like a fountain. The column of acid almost touched the roof of the dragon's stomach before it crashed back down, spattering the boat.

"Ow!" Anil cried, wiping at his arm.

A sharp stinging on Alex's neck quickened to a sizzling burn. Kraken shot a jet of clean water to wash it away and soothe the pain.

"Uh oh." Beside them, Zoey had lifted her eyes to the roof. She turned pale. "The ceiling is moving."

Alex followed her gaze. Above the tideline of algae, he had thought there was nothing but dark flesh. But the geyser hadn't only affected them. Parasites scurried away from where the acid had sprayed. There were enough of them that they had *become* the roof of the stomach, their transparent armour rendering them invisible until they moved. Now the light gleamed on insectile armour and flexing legs as the parasites – too many to count – skittered towards the island of salt.

Ready to drop between them and the way out.

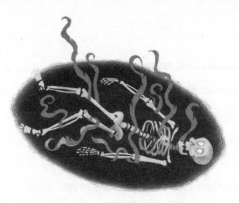

CHAPTER TWENTY-FIVE

SKULL AND BONES

A hard tug on the strap brought Zoey's seafire backpack flaring to life. Seafire light filled the boat, sealing them once again inside a protective bubble. The parasites above their heads screeched but kept flooding towards the island of salt.

"Maybe we should go back," Alex said.

"No." Callis drove the oars harder through the swamp. "They'll follow us whichever way we go."

Through his jacket, Alex touched the bottle of poison Argosy had given him. Maybe there was a way to use it against the parasites? But he might hurt the dragon at the same time...

Instead of taking them directly across the stomach, Callis aimed their boat at the island.

"Where are we going?" Alex asked.

Callis strained with the effort of rowing. "I know what I'm doing!"

By the time the rowing boat scraped up onto the island, the salt was crawling with parasites. This time, the abominable creatures didn't swarm. They moved more carefully, as if they had learned to fear the blistering kiss of the light, spreading out to surround the landing group.

Alex reached down into his well of power, ready to draw it up at the first sign of attack. Zoey and Anil appeared similarly braced, though they had no weapons. It would be impossible to fight so many of the monsters, but he knew they would try.

"Keep moving," Callis ordered.

The salt crunched underfoot like iced-over snow as they climbed out of the boat. The ground was pocked and pitted, debris sticking out at treacherous angles and lurking in pools of acid.

Callis immediately marched into the lead, abandoning the shoreline and heading uphill.

"Is that the right way?" Zoey asked.

Anil studied the landscape like a tactician. "If we go onto high ground, they might trap us."

"It's faster to go up and over than around the edge," Callis replied gruffly, without breaking stride.

There was no choice but to follow or allow him to stray out of the light. The parasites tracked them patiently, maintaining a close circle around the group. There wasn't enough space for them all on the ground, so some leaped deftly from rock to salty stalagmite, debris to junk, making sure to avoid the pools of acid water.

Callis led them around the side of the severed ship. The wood was rimed with salt, seaweed covering gaps broken in the hull. The ground continued to slope upwards, leading them past the mangled mast. The remains of the ship were broken over a steep mound of salt, a flat stretch of deck lying above them.

"Even if we get across the stomach," Anil said, "how do we stop the parasites following us?"

Callis hadn't revealed this part of the plan. Usually, there was a trick up his sleeve. Alex hoped that desperation hadn't made the pirate reckless.

A bulging bubble in the swamp below caught his eye. It swelled from the water, dilating into an enormous blister.

Another geyser.

The bubble burst, a torrent of water erupting from underneath.

"Look out!" Alex shouted.

The plume of fizzing water was strong enough to rise above the mound of salt, threatening to wash over their heads. Alex swiped his hands sideways, magic pouring out of him automatically. The connection between him and the Water Dragon flexed, a trickle of power moving along it.

The geyser folded sideways as if Alex had physically slapped it. Water sprayed over the parasites instead, knocking them from their perches and washing over their armoured backs. The creatures screeched and tried to lurch away, falling over each other.

"Yes!" cheered Zoey.

The broken column of water sank away, acid streaming down the slope of the salt.

Alex felt his own stomach sink. Parasites lifted themselves from the draining water. Smoke trailed from their shells, acid gnawing ragged holes in their transparent armour, but the creatures clicked back to their feet as if simply emerging from a hot bath.

"They're too strong," Anil said.

Kraken curled two arms into fists and shook them at the parasites.

Alex refused to feel disheartened, even as the parasites regrouped to surround them once again. A storm of power was brewing inside him. His connection to the dragon was suddenly singing.

"Do you feel that?" asked Zoey.

"I think the dragon is trying to—" Alex began to say.

"Hurry up!" Callis hissed. The interruption was harsher than mere impatience. A desperate hunger burned in the pirate's eyes that Alex had seen there twice before – both times Alex had needed to stop him.

They stumbled up the mound of salt, propelling Zoey between them to ensure they all remained inside the light. The parasites followed, shells sizzling with acid.

Finally, they drew level with the deck of the wrecked ship. The wood was mostly hollowed out by decay, leaving deep pools and chasms that brimmed with water and bristled with swallowed junk. A shopping trolley jutted from a crooked fracture, its nose twisted and blackened by acid. A string of shattered gas lanterns, a type not used for a hundred years, trailed from a lopsided spur.

"What are the chances I can come back and get this stuff later?" Zoey asked.

Anil peered over the edge of the deck. It was a sheer drop to the acid swamp below. The parasites blocked any escape back the way they had come. "We need to worry about getting out of here at all."

Callis picked his way across the deck as quickly as he could. He hardly seemed to notice the parasites now, although they crept into the light as close as they dared, mandibles snapping in anticipation.

"It's here somewhere..." the pirate muttered, eyes sweeping the rotten wood.

"An unlikely but ultimately exciting and successful way out of this seemingly impossible situation?" Anil asked.

Alex's skin prickled as if he had rolled through dry seaweed. A voice whispered at the back of his mind. A familiar language – waves lapping at rocks, birds wheeling above a shoal of fish, sails creaking in the wind. The language of sea magic. But it spoke too quickly to be understood, whispers collapsing into themselves, the words garbled.

"Here!" Callis called, beckoning them after him.

In the middle of the deck, the wood had collapsed into a deep pool crusted with salt. The water was murky, yet somehow glowed faintly red. Magic seemed to brim there. It felt different to the magic Alex held inside him. This power was unstable, impatient, itching to break free.

The frantic whisper raked at Alex's mind as he stepped closer. It was like approaching a wild animal, unsure if it might lash out. Kraken's skin flashed red in warning, the same colour as the pool, the octopus tugging at his collar to try and hold him back. Even the parasites sensed it, backing off a little.

Whatever lurked inside the pool, it was not their friend. Alex knew it as the malevolent voice threatened to overwhelm him, howling inside his mind. He wanted to run, get as far away from it as he could.

"We should keep moving," he said, voice shaking as he tried to hide his panic.

The precipice of the deck offered a sweeping view across the cavernous stomach. Beyond the rest of the swamp was a shadowy stretch of wall where Alex hoped they would find an exit.

Callis climbed over the edge of the pool until he was as close to the water as he could get. He scanned its surface while rolling up his sleeves.

"It'll burn you," Zoey said.

"What's a little more pain?"

Callis plunged his arms into the water. Immediately, his skin sizzled. He gritted his teeth and delved deeper until he was up to his shoulders.

"What are you looking for?" Anil asked, covering his nose from the smell.

"We'll take the light and leave you," Alex threatened.

"It won't matter." Callis grunted. "It's here. I saw it."

The pirate finally seemed to find what he sought in the pool. His face lit up and he threw his weight backwards to heave something clear of the water.

The raving voice grew so loud that Alex held his head and stumbled back. Behind them, the parasites lifted their heads and clacked their mandibles together in an excited frenzy.

It was a human skeleton. Bones yellow and gnawed but still intact, skull grinning, strands of seaweed filling the gaps between teeth. The bones glowed red, wild and twisted magic holding the skeleton together, flying from it strongly enough to almost knock Alex off his feet.

Callis dragged the skeleton onto the salt, the skin of his arms blistered red from the burning acid.

Alex's heart hammered against his ribs, the rancorous voice bludgeoning inside his head. Standing close to the skeleton felt like bracing himself against a howling gale.

"Who is that?" he asked through gritted teeth.

Callis smirked, wider and wider, until he broke into wild laughter.

"I'm not the only member of my family to be swallowed by the Water Dragon!"

In one quick movement, Callis popped the skeleton's grinning skull off its neck and held it up to face them.

"I'm honoured to introduce you to my most famous ancestor," he said. "Brineblood himself."

CHAPTER TWENTY-SIX

ANY CHANCE IT'S NOT A BETRAYAL?

The grinning skull radiated feral sea magic, the purity of the Water Dragon's power twisted into sinister, frightful form.

Its voice screamed inside Alex's head, though its rotten jaw remained closed in a grin. A wave of seasickness made his throat tighten and his vision blur.

Where he touched the skull, Callis's skin began to glow. Red sparks ricocheted up his arms and wiped away the livid burns, healing them as if they had never been there at all.

"It can't be Brineblood." Alex shook his head, trying not to be sick.

Anil studied the skull. "The story says he was swallowed hundreds of years ago. It *looks* old enough."

Callis smiled exultantly as magic skittered across his skin.

"I spotted it here when the dragon swallowed me. Still lying in its final resting place after all this time. I tried to reach it through the tumult of the churning acid but it was too dangerous."

He paused to peer across the wide swamp of acid that stretched beneath the precipice of the broken ship's deck. The parasites crowded at the edge of the light.

"When I returned to try and retrieve the bones, I couldn't find a way across the acid. And then the parasites arrived to make it doubly impossible."

"Until you found us," Alex said. "And convinced us to help you."

Callis grinned wolfishly. "I always could find a way to make you do my dirty work."

Anger churned through the seasickness in Alex's belly. He should have known that even in a place like this, where it seemed mere survival should surpass any notion of a villainous plot, Callis would find a way to indulge his insatiable appetite for power.

"We're not great at learning from our mistakes, are we?" Anil mused.

"It doesn't make sense," Zoey argued. "The acid should easily have dissolved the skeleton into broth by now."

Callis beamed at the skull like a proud parent. "Brineblood was bonded to the Water Dragon. Even after their connection was broken, I wondered if his bones remembered the power they held. It must have protected them while they lay here for centuries, soaking up the dragon's magic. Making them stronger than Brineblood could ever have dreamed."

"So it was never just about retrieving your ancestor's remains," Alex said. "You think you've finally found a way to claim sea magic for yourself."

Zoey winced. "Is there any chance you're going to use the power of the gross old skeleton to help us, rather than take revenge and sabotage our really important plan?"

Callis squeezed Brineblood's skull in his hand. The manic voice intensified inside Alex's head as power fizzed free of the bone. Callis's fingers glowed. The pirate barked a laugh, gaping in ravenous disbelief at his own hands.

"I didn't think so." Zoey sighed.

Alex reached for his magic in response. But the frenzied voice chattered in his mind, making seasickness lurch through his belly once more. The magic slipped out of reach. The skull blocked his power, just like the parasites had blocked his connection to the infected animals.

Callis grinned. "Now you'll see."

He swept a luminous arm downwards and slapped the murky surface of the pool. The magic scattered like shrapnel from his hand and lifted the acid into a furious wave, forcing them to duck as it sprayed over their heads and sizzled on the deck.

"He missed!" Anil crowed.

Kraken tugged Alex's hair to pull him upright and pointed frantically. Callis hadn't missed – the wave of acid had been a distraction so he could grab Zoey. Now he dragged her, kicking and squirming, to the edge of the deck, the long fall to the swamp just behind them.

"You thought I'd died in here," Callis said. "Now I'll make that your fate instead." Callis jerked his elbow against Zoey's backpack, smashing the seafire light into pieces. "Maybe you'll live long enough to retrieve her bones."

"Alex," Zoey said, voice shaking.

Callis tugged the backpack and tipped her over the edge of the cliff.

"No!" Alex bellowed, he and Anil scrambling forwards. They ignored Callis darting in the opposite direction, Brineblood's skull clutched in his grip. The parasites flinched away from the power of the skull, opening a path for Callis to escape.

Alex and Anil reached the edge of the deck in time to see Zoey falling towards the acid swamp. Alex threw out a desperate hand, but the taint of the skull's twisted power still blocked his magic. He could only watch his friend fall.

Zoey splashed into the deadly acid.

And bounced.

Alex gaped in disbelief as a bubble swelled beneath her, cushioning her body like a pillow, a barrier between her and the swamp.

"Nice catch," breathed Anil.

"That wasn't me."

Sea magic surged, washing away the twisted force of the skull. Alex couldn't tell where it came from.

The bubble beneath Zoey burst. A geyser erupted underneath her, throwing her screaming into the air. But instead of being engulfed by the boiling acid, she stayed perfectly balanced on top, one hand held out with fingers spread as she drew level with the deck.

Alex's jaw dropped open. *She* was where the magic was coming from.

"Hi, guys," Zoey said, surfing on the geyser top. "I think I'm magic now."

CHAPTER TWENTY-SEVEN

MANY MAGICS

The top of the geyser was crusted with salt, a solid platform that protected Zoey from the acid. She held the water in a constant stream underneath her feet.

"How are you doing that?" Alex asked.

"It feels a bit like wetting myself through my fingers," Zoey called back. She pointed behind them. "I think you might want to join me."

Now the backpack light and the skull's erratic magic were gone, the parasites had regrouped. They swarmed over the broken deck, quickly closing the gap to pin Alex and Anil against the edge of the precipice. Kraken flared red and fired bullets of water, but it did nothing to deter the parasites' advance.

Alex grabbed Anil and they jumped together onto the teetering top of the geyser.

"Now what?" Anil asked.

Zoey turned and extended a hand above the swamp below. Around them, the algae on the walls shimmered brighter. Alex felt a surge of magic. Fragile and desperate. Beyond Zoey, another geyser fountained from the swamp and hovered within reach.

"The dragon is too weak to help us directly," Alex said, "so it's given you sea magic instead."

"What about me?" Anil threw a hand back towards the pursuing parasites. Nothing happened. "That doesn't seem fair."

There was no time to console him. The second geyser offered a stepping stone and they leaped across, Zoey already summoning another.

The parasites screeched and tumbled onto the first geyser. As soon as their armoured feet touched the salt platform it broke apart, sending the creatures tumbling into the acid below.

"What does it feel like?" Anil asked, after they had jumped to the next geyser.

"I've felt the power inside me since we entered the dragon. I just needed the right nudge to connect with it." Zoey smiled. "I think you have it too. Maybe you just need to be moments from certain death before you can access it."

Behind them, the parasites abandoned trying to follow the geyser path and now swarmed up the walls instead, scrambling towards the ceiling to give chase.

"You'd really think this would be enough," Anil said.

The next geyser was slower to rise, the water stuttering upwards under its own weight. Zoey strained, sweat pouring down her face. Alex put a hand on her shoulder and let his magic flow. Their power mingled together as naturally as if they had always shared it. The geyser surged into place.

"Where are we actually going?" Anil shouted.

The tottering path had brought them close to the edge of the stomach. As if the dragon had overheard, the fleshy wall ahead twitched and a valve opened up to receive them.

"There!"

The salt crackled under their feet as they jumped to the next geyser. Below, Alex caught a glimpse of Callis in the wooden rowing boat, Brineblood's skull glowing red as he used its power to propel himself to safety.

"We'll get him," Zoey spat.

Alex definitely wouldn't want to mess with her now she had sea magic at her fingertips.

The parasites pressed forward across the roof,

threatening to reach the far side of the stomach first and cut them off.

"Just a little further," Alex said.

One more geyser would get them close enough to jump for the exit. Alex and Zoey combined their strength to tease it up from the swamp. This time, Anil dropped his hand onto Zoey's other shoulder.

Power gushed. It seemed to blow the lid off their magic completely, throwing them wide open to each other. The power wasn't divided between them. It didn't just belong to the dragon. It was a single force, an unbreakable connection they all shared.

"I feel it!" Anil shouted.

Instead of holding firm, the geyser surged upwards to fling them all into the air. They flew into the waiting escape tunnel, parasite mandibles snapping at them as they passed, before the valve closed up and sealed the thwarted monsters on the other side.

The darkness made it nearly impossible to know if they were travelling in the right direction or if any further hazard lurked ahead. The backpack light had offered more than protection; it had allowed them to press towards their goal without delay.

Still, they waded on through ankle deep sludge, sticking together so nobody could fall behind. A stifling, metallic odour wafted up from the gunk and the air grew clammily warm.

"I always thought you were milking the whole *tired-after-using-magic* thing," Zoey panted. "But I'm *exhausted*."

Alex wiped sweat from his forehead. His legs were almost too heavy to lift.

"Let's find dry ground so we can rest."

The sludgy trudge continued for what felt like hours but might have only been minutes. Finally, the sludge grew shallower until it was only squelching underfoot. They leaned against the side of the pipe to catch their breath.

"I did magic!" Anil turned his hands over in disbelief. "We both did!"

Zoey smiled, before trying to hide it.

"You were both incredible," Alex said. "We wouldn't have got out of there without you."

Sheepishly, Zoey met his eye. "You don't mind that we have magic too?"

"Why would I mind?" Alex supposed he *could* see why she would worry. But he had never thought of the magic as something that belonged to him. It was a blessing shared with him by the dragon because it believed he was worthy. It was no surprise at all that his friends were worthy too!

"I'm glad it's not just me any more."

"Okay, good, because that was awesome!" Zoey high-fived Anil hard enough to make him wince. "But why now?"

"We know the Water Dragon has bonded with people and shared its magic before. That's how Brineblood and Alex's grandma got their powers," Anil said. "After everything we've all been through together, it must have bonded with us too."

Zoey poked a finger into the shallow sludge and tried to force her magic out, creating little more than a burping ripple. "It felt a lot easier to use it when I thought I was going to die."

Anil smiled and threw out an arm, flexing his fingers dramatically. Nothing happened. "Maybe you can train us?"

"Of course I will." Though Alex wasn't quite sure *how* he would teach them. "For now, we have to get on with the mission."

A familiar sound fuzzed from Zoey's backpack. She scrambled to open it and retrieve the walkie-talkie.

"*Do you receive me?*" Meri's voice crackled from the speaker.

"Doctor Dragon receiving, over!" Zoey said back.

"*I've been trying to get through for ages! Is everything all right? We've been watching the storm wall for any signs of change. About an hour ago it started to weaken.*"

Alex reached for the dragon along their frayed connection. Through the dark, smothering energy of the blighting parasites, he could feel the well of its power running dry. It wouldn't be able to fight for much longer.

"We're close to the brain," Zoey said, though she sounded uncertain. "There's still time."

"*Hurry. And stay safe!*" Meri chuckled to acknowledge it might not be possible to do both. "*Now the storm wall is weaker, we're moving closer, so we'll be ready to pick you up as soon as it's done.*"

"Keep the engine running," Zoey said.

"*We don't have an engine, the ship is entirely—*"

"Figure of speech!" Zoey shut off the walkie-talkie. "I'm going to mix up as much cure as I can while Anil works out where we're going."

"We can't even see." Anil turned hopefully to Kraken, perched reliably on Alex's shoulder. "Octopuses are bioluminescent, right? Maybe she can light our way!"

Kraken picked herself up and flexed her arms as if straining with all her might. Although her skin rapidly cycled through colours – blue, green, yellow, orange – it offered no light.

"*Some* octopuses produce light," Alex corrected, stroking her head reassuringly. "Not this species."

Kraken refused to accept failure. Straining harder, her

241

eyes bulged and legs curled. Her body rippled and a heavy splatter of black ink splashed onto Alex's shoulder.

"That was a different kind of enlightening." Anil dipped his pen into the ink and scribbled in his notebook.

After Zoey had mixed more of the cure, they began fumbling their way along the passage, sludge once again sucking at their ankles.

"Do you think Callis is going to come after us?" Anil asked as he led the way. "I know he could never beat us before. But now he's got the power of Brineblood's skull."

Zoey squinted ahead into the dark. "Maybe he thinks the parasites will finish us off. He's used to letting other people do the hard work."

Thankfully, they hadn't encountered any more parasites since their narrow escape from the dragon's stomach. If – when? – they did, at least there would be three of them with magic to fend the monsters off.

"We can't let Callis distract us. He only cares about escaping," Alex said. "We can deal with him later."

"If we ever find our way out of here," Zoey grumbled.

A shudder ran through the wall of the passage. A deep booming sound followed it like distant thunder.

"What the heck was that?" asked Zoey.

Anil groaned. "I wish we could go five minutes without something bad happening."

"It's not bad." Alex pushed past them. The sludge squelched beneath his feet. Zoey and Anil followed.

The passage shook again. The pursuing rumble was louder this time and doubled like a drumbeat: *boo-boom*.

"Ha!" Zoey exclaimed.

Anil brandished his fists, ready to fight. "What is it?"

"It's the dragon's heartbeat." A smile broke across Alex's face. "We're close enough that we can hear it."

The next *thump-thump* left them awestruck. It reverberated through the walls and inside their chests.

"That's what we're fighting to save," Alex said. "The Water Dragon has spent centuries being attacked and hunted. Fighting to protect the oceans against a relentless tide of abuse. Even now, it doesn't give up."

One hand strayed to his pocket, where the vial of Argosy's poison was still hidden.

"As long as that heart is beating, we have to do everything we can to help."

Anil beamed. "And now we know we're going the right way."

Zoey glanced at the messy map he'd been sketching. "How?"

"If we're close to its heart, we must be moving up the dragon's body." Anil pointed ahead. "We can use its heartbeat to help us navigate."

He led the way, pushing quickly in pursuit of the heartbeat. Each resounding *boo-boom* seemed to chase the ache from their legs. Gradually, the direction of the sound shifted. It grew closer for a while, before steadily falling behind, spurring them forwards with every beat.

"The ground is sloping," Anil said, breathing hard.

Almost imperceptibly, the sludge dried up completely. The dragon's heartbeat fell further behind and the incline grew more severe. Soon they were taking exaggerated steps to tackle the steep angle.

"It's coiling," Zoey said. "We're going around like a spiral staircase."

Alex remembered the strange, coiled shape of the Water Dragon cocooned inside the storm. The whorls of its coils had grown tighter higher up its body, as if it were holding itself close for protection. Lower in its body, inside the looser curls, the ascent hadn't been so obvious. Now the spiralling incline couldn't be missed.

They climbed for a long while, legs burning, pushing themselves as hard as they could. Finally, an arch of light appeared ahead. The ground flattened and they emerged inside a vast domed chamber.

Alex, Zoey and Anil leaned on their knees to catch their breath. It took Kraken tugging impatiently on his hair for Alex to look up.

The Water Dragon's brain stretched out overhead like an enormous sculpture. Two long, wrinkled lobes of grey flesh folding back on itself in an elegant swoop. Webs of delicate veins crackled with electricity across its surface.

They had finally reached their goal. Inside the dragon's skull. It should have been a spectacular sight.

Instead, they stared up in horror.

Parasite eggs covered the entire underside of the dragon's brain. Yellow beads the size of cannon balls nestled together in thick, slimy clumps, trailing strings of yellow ooze. Parasites lingered nearby, bristling at the arrival of invaders but staying close to their eggs.

Zoey fumbled for her backpack. "We have to use the antidote."

"It's too late."

Sickness lurched in Alex's belly as he gazed up at the impossibly huge nest. Everywhere, the eggs began to wobble, creatures stirring inside them. Popping and cracking sounds filled the air as sharp legs and ravenous mandibles broke the shells.

"They're already hatching."

CHAPTER TWENTY-EIGHT

PARASITES LOST

It couldn't all have been for nothing. Against the odds they had found a way inside the Water Dragon and harvested precious zircongris to create the cure. They had fought so hard to traverse the dragon's body and reach the source of infection.

Only to arrive too late.

"There are thousands of them," Anil said. "Maybe more."

The cure was designed to work fastest on unhatched eggs. Although it could destroy live parasites too, surely there would simply be too many now they were hatching. The dragon would still be infected and more parasites would swarm out into the world.

The eggs continued to crack open, shards of broken

shell dropping around them like peeling paint. A cacophony of screeching and creaking bludgeoned the air as insectile limbs unfolded for the first time, transparent armour plates hardening into place. Some babies were almost as large as their parents while others were the size of ants, crawling over the backs of their larger siblings.

"There has to be a way we can still stop them," Alex said, refusing to acknowledge the pit of hopelessness opening in his gut.

"We didn't come all this way not to even try." Zoey retrieved two large jars of the cure from her bag. Then she pointed. "There!"

The dragon's brain stem trailed from the infested organ, a thick bundle of nerve tissue that dropped into a circular pool of fluid at the top of the dragon's spine. Zoey opened the jars and emptied every drop of cure into the pool.

The luminous green liquid spread quickly, lighting up the fluid with cleansing light.

"Quickly!" Zoey thrust a hand into the water. "We can use our power to spread it."

Alex and Anil dipped their hands into the glowing fluid. Together, they pushed with their shared magic as hard as they could.

The fluid kicked up into a stormy wave, frothing against the dragon's skull as it rose higher and higher, before it broke to wash over the infested brain.

It spread like green fire, rolling flames across the surface of the dragon's brain. Unhatched eggs splintered and shrivelled as soon as it touched them, great clumps melting into paste. The parasites screeched and recoiled as the purifying fire advanced.

"It's like seafire," Zoey said. "It only hurts them."

Eggs continued to hatch despite the approaching fire. Parasites old and new leaped away from the brain, evading the sweeping green tide. There were simply too many of them. The flames spread along the walls, descending into the dragon's body. The only way for the parasites to survive it was to escape the dragon all together. They began to swarm towards the back of its skull.

"They're heading for the dragon's mouth," Anil said. "The same way we need to go."

"There has to be something else we can do!" Alex cast around helplessly.

"At least we've thinned the parasites' numbers!" Zoey shoved them both along. "If we can escape ahead of the parasites, we've bought enough time to regroup with the others and come up with a new plan."

Reluctantly, Alex joined his friends in running deeper inside the dragon's skull, parasites alive and dead tumbling around them as the wave of green fire finished washing across the dragon's brain. Alex tucked Kraken inside his jacket so no smaller monster would infect her.

Stabbing sickness made him briefly stumble. Brineblood's magic blew through him like a gale from somewhere nearby. That meant Callis was close. But there was no time to worry about him now.

"Get on the radio," Alex instructed. "Tell Meri we're coming out and we're not alone."

Static fuzzed from the walkie-talkie as Zoey clicked it awake. "Taxi, please!"

The reply was muffled but instant. "*We're already close. We'll pick you up.*"

"The parasites have hatched," Zoey told her. "We'll have to get away fast and find a plan B."

The dragon's skull curved down behind its brain. A gap between bone and sinew offered a way down. Jumping into it without hesitation, they tumbled down a bumpy chute that looped lower inside the dragon's head. Parasites poured after them, screeching and snapping.

The chute spat them out into a hot, dark space and they rolled across a wet, prickly carpet. Tall, yellow spires rose in regular rows to either side.

Tongue and teeth.

They were inside the dragon's mouth.

Somebody cursed and Alex was hauled roughly to his feet.

"Fancy meeting you here."

Callis held Alex with one hand and the skull of his ancestor with the other. The skull's power lashed at Alex's senses, filling his head with thunder, making his stomach lurch as if he stood on the deck of a ship in high wind.

Zoey and Anil sprang upright behind Alex. Callis squared himself, red magic trailing over his skin, ready for a fight. But the screech of parasites inside the chute cut the confrontation short.

"Fancy helping me fight them off?" Callis asked.

Alex almost laughed. "I'm not falling for that again."

The dragon's tongue was spongy under their running feet. Its monumental jaws stayed firmly shut on either side of its mouth.

"If the dragon doesn't open up, we'll be trapped!" Anil shouted.

The feet of the pursuing parasites drummed on the wet flesh of the dragon's tongue. Behind them, green fire swept down the chute from the dragon's brain, herding the monsters ahead of it.

They had needed to escape before the parasites reached the exit, but the monsters were too fast.

Alex swept a hand down towards a puddle of salty saliva and pushed with his magic. The water became a wave that swept fiercely towards their pursuers. But Callis squeezed

Brineblood's skull and lifted a halting palm. The wave was dashed to pieces.

"You won't get me that easily!" he crowed.

"I was aiming for the parasites, you idiot!" Alex shouted back.

The sealed end of the Water Dragon's mouth was fast approaching. Cracks of sunlight squeezed through narrow gaps between its front teeth, nowhere near wide enough for them to slip through.

The group, along with Callis, screeched to a halt and whirled around. A line of the largest parasites led a pulsing swarm of smaller progeny, tumbling over itself like a wave. The green flames rolled steadily after them.

"Why isn't your blasted dragon opening up?" Callis demanded. "We're doomed if we stay here!"

"But if the dragon lets us out, it also lets out the parasites," Alex said.

It wouldn't be enough to destroy every parasite in the dragon's body, but the rolling fire would take out most of the monsters trapped inside its mouth. That was more important than escaping.

Swallowing a lump in his throat, Alex looked to his friends. They had already sacrificed so much. Now both Zoey and Anil simply smiled in solidarity and took each other's hands as they faced the parasites being herded towards them by the green fire.

Callis lashed out at the monsters with his volatile magic, but there were simply too many. Instead, he turned around and began physically trying to prise the dragon's mouth open.

"And he thinks *we're* the stupid ones," muttered Zoey.

A fumbling sound came through the walkie-talkie as if somebody was wrestling for its control. The voice that came through was strained and breathing hard.

"*The poison!*" Argosy shouted. "*You have to use it!*"

"What's he talking about?" Anil asked.

Kraken recoiled as Alex took the bottle of thick black liquid from his pocket. "Argosy gave me poison to give the dragon as a last resort. I never even thought about using it. But now I can't make this decision by myself. If we use the poison, it doesn't just stop the Water Dragon's power being turned against the world. It also gives us a chance to get out of here alive."

Anil's eyes were wide with horror. "How could he...? No, even if it would work, it's not *right*."

Zoey answered by snatching the poison away and shoving it inside her jacket. "Not in a million years."

Alex nodded, feeling a wave of relief despite everything. Then he tried to reach for the dragon. Before, the connection had been smothered by the parasites' infection. Now it flickered faintly with life. Destroying the eggs must have opened up the connection again.

Hold them here as long as you can, Alex thought, hoping the dragon could still hear him. *Don't worry about us.*

If there was a response, it was lost under a barrage of chattering, feral magic from Brineblood's skull. Callis gripped the bone and sent red tendrils snapping at the dragon's teeth and snaking around its jaw. Slowly, the dark magic began to prise open the dragon's mouth.

"No!" Alex shouted. "Don't let them out!"

"I didn't come all this way to die here!" Callis roared.

The parasites had almost reached them, the green fire of the cure swamping those at the back.

A groan resounded from deep inside the dragon. The sound rose up from beneath their feet, rumbling through muscle and bone. At their backs, daylight poured inside as the dragon's mouth opened wider. Brineblood's magic had started the job, but now the dragon was taking control.

Alex, Zoey and Anil wrapped their arms around a tooth to hold on tight as the dragon tipped its head backwards. Parasites screeched as their feet scrabbled for grip, some tumbling away into the fire.

The quake intensified like thunder rolling across a horizon. Air rushed past them as the rising sound grew louder, and louder, until there was nothing but deafening noise.

The Water Dragon opened its mouth wide and *roared*.

Alex held the tooth tightly so the gusting exhalation wouldn't blow him loose. He spotted Anil and Zoey doing the same, eyes clenched shut against the force of the roar. Only Callis watched, already searching for an escape.

Finally, the dragon lowered its head. But its mouth stayed open. Daylight flooded inside. Alex peered out between the dragon's teeth at the long drop to the churning ocean below. He spotted *The Dragonfly*, sails snapping as it wheeled in front of the dragon.

Parasites were already scurrying for the exit. Callis didn't hesitate. He threw Alex a smug salute and stepped over the edge of the dragon's mouth. They watched him fall for a long time before losing sight of him in the mist thrown up by the turbulent sea.

"We have to do that too, don't we?" Anil said.

Zoey nodded. "No point staying here now the dragon's opened up."

Teetering at the edge of the dragon's mouth, they peered down at the great height between them and the relative safety of *The Dragonfly*'s deck.

"On three?" suggested Anil.

Alex nodded, hoping his thundering heartbeat wouldn't disturb his ability to count. "One, two—"

He gasped as Zoey tipped them all forwards before he

could finish the count. They tumbled out between the dragon's teeth, into empty air, the torrid ocean rushing up to meet them.

CHAPTER TWENTY-NINE

THE TIDE OF BATTLE

Rain lashed Alex's skin, hard as bullets, as he fell, wind rushing in his ears. Scaled coils whipped past as he plunged through a loop of the Water Dragon's body. Eyes streaming, Alex glimpsed the full enclosure of the captive storm. It had weakened as the dragon's strength waned, but walls of dark cloud still boiled high above crashing waves and snaps of lightning.

The view diminished as Alex closed on the frothing ocean around the base of the dragon. *The Dragonfly* battled the wind to stay close by, figures hurrying around the deck.

Alex held out his arms as if ready to catch himself, casting around for something to latch onto with his magic. He couldn't grasp the stinging rain, and the ocean, despite growing rapidly closer, was too far away to summon. Magic sputtered from his fingers like electricity along a loose connection.

Instead, he reached out to where Zoey and Anil fell beside him. Zoey and Anil stretched out their arms and their magic connected, flowing freely and easily between them. Another source reached up to them from below, completing the circuit. Together, they thrust their arms towards it just before they crashed down.

Water closed around Alex's body, dampening the noise of the storm. Bitter cold knocked the breath from his body.

But there was no impact. No sudden jarring stop. No pain. Alex's descent simply slowed. Magic nipped at his skin, singing a single sweet note that cut clearly through the clamour of the storm.

Then he was whisked sideways, closing on a familiar shape made blurry by the water.

Oof.

Alex landed hard on sodden, mismatched wood. Blinking water from his eyes, he lifted his head to find Bridget and Grandpa standing over him.

"I am *not* touching you until you've had a shower," his sister said.

The baby dragon was suspended above them in its harness to keep it clear of the infected water, scales glowing green, juvenile ruff inflated with effort. That had been the source of magic from below! It had used its power to help catch him from the sky.

Two waterspouts tottered towards *The Dragonfly* and folded over the deck. Zoey and Anil spilled out of them into a heap.

Grandpa pulled Alex to his feet and enveloped him in a hug. "Yer made it back. I knew yer would."

The otters – still wearing their hats – nosed enquiringly around his legs, Chonkers joining them to sniff at the strange smells. Meri and Gene helped the others to their feet.

"Where's the *Dorothea*?" Alex asked.

"We left her outside the storm wall," Grandpa said. "No point riskin' both ships gettin' destroyed."

Reluctantly, Alex pulled out of the hug to peer up at the Water Dragon, its head looming impossibly high above the ship. Its mouth gaped open and parasites crawled over its lips. The creatures scuttled along the spines of its chin and began their descent down its body. "We took out some of the parasites. But not enough."

"I should have known you wouldn't have the courage to do what was needed." Argosy stepped from the shadows at the back of the crowd. "You could have stopped this!"

Zoey marched up to the old man and shoved the bottle of black poison into his hands. "And we should have known you would never learn the difference between doing the right thing and the easy thing."

Argosy's face flushed red as he inflated with indignation. He looked for support from Anil, who simply set his mouth into a hard line and firmly shook his head.

"We should at least get the baby dragon away before it's too late!" Argosy insisted.

Nobody moved, *The Dragonfly*'s crew waiting for their captain's order.

"Bring us back around," Meri instructed. "There must still be something we can do. If you thinned out some of the parasites, there might be an opening for you and the baby dragon to combine your magic and try—"

The ship jolted, hull groaning, as if it had been struck. Voices rose in panic further along the deck. A young crewman ran to report to his captain, the front of his shirt ripped.

"Infected animals are storming the ship."

Feet drummed on the deck, interspersed with agitated clicking and wet slapping on the wood. Crew spilled backwards in retreat, falling over each other in their haste to escape. A sea lion was first to lumber into view, long neck arched high, whiskery snout twitching as its lips peeled back over sharp, black teeth. Lobsters flanked its flat front flippers, oversized red and blue mottled claws snapping, crabs forming a sideways cavalry behind them. Sea snakes slithered across the deck between the scaly flippers of sea turtles.

All had eyes flat and cold as wet shale. Alex extended his magic towards them and felt the connection stifled.

The Dragonfly juddered again. Over the railing, Alex saw the vast shadow of a whale preparing to ram the hull. Dolphins, stingrays and teeming schools of fish swirled around it.

The parasites had rallied their full forces for the battle. Turned friends into foes. Ready to try and take over the ocean for good.

Above them, the Water Dragon roared. The cure had been delivered too late to wipe out the parasites completely. But it had taken out some and forced others to relinquish their control and flee. While the parasites were regrouping, there was an opening. A chance the Water Dragon could use the dregs of its power to push back against the infection. It would use every last drop of its strength to fight the parasites.

Alex and his friends would do the same.

"Protect the baby dragon!" he shouted.

Meri and Gene quickly handed out a selection of makeshift weapons: oars and boat hooks, mops and brooms, lengths of rope with heavy knots tied at their ends. Bridget refused to take anything, crunching her neck side to side and shaking out her arms.

"Get them off the ship!" Meri bellowed. "Try not to hurt them!"

"Shame they en't gonna do us the same favour," Grandpa grumbled, brandishing a mop.

There was no time to organize. The infected animals charged, flippers and claws thundering across the deck.

The crew of *The Dragonfly* rose to meet them. Instead of striking their attackers, they swept their weapons across the deck like hockey sticks, bumping lobsters through the drainage gaps in the railing and spinning turtles away like pucks.

The otters teamed up with Chonkers to form a half circle around the sea lion and block its path. It snapped at them clumsily, the otters easily dancing out of reach. This created an opening for Chonkers to leap onto the sea lion's back and cinch her paws tightly around its neck to bring it down.

"Yer make a great team!" Grandpa shouted to them.

Pinch swept down from the sky, wings braced against the squalling wind, and launched a heavy rock to bowl across the deck and knock crabs flying. Then he plucked up a wriggling sea snake in his beak and tossed it into the ocean before circling around to strike again.

Alex took a deep breath, trying to stay calm. He imagined the magic inside himself as a deep, placid pool (a task made harder by Kraken arching to spit bullets of water from his shoulder). Zoey and Anil stood beside him. Alex reached up to the baby dragon suspended above the deck, panicked eyes darting around the battle.

"It's going to be okay." Alex rested a hand on the dragon's dewy scales. Zoey and Anil reached up too. The bond with his friends was powerful, whether or not they had control of their sea magic. Overhead, power flared from the Water Dragon, a blazing beacon in the sky, as it fought against the control of the parasites.

Another shuddering blow struck *The Dragonfly*, a wounded groan keening through its timbers. The ship reeled sideways, allowing a wave to broadside them. The deck tipped steeply and staggered the battling crew.

The sea lion righted itself onto its flippers and butted a nearby crewwoman hard enough to throw her overboard. Snakes shimmied up the shaft of Grandpa's mop, entangling his hands. Meri tried to shake crabs off her oar before their weight dragged it from her grip. Lobsters had managed to hitch a ride on Bridget's arms and pinched viciously while Gene tried to knock them off. A wave washed more animals up onto the deck, driving the crew back towards the baby dragon.

Alex pressed his fingers firmly to the baby dragon's scales. Magic harmonized between them, singing between him and his friends. Alex pictured a bright sunbeam cutting through the storm, lighting their way, and he knew the dragon and his friends saw it too. More than their power banded them together – it was their *purpose*.

The baby dragon's ruff inflated. Together, Alex, Zoey and Anil lifted their free hands. Magic coursed through them.

Enough water misted the air and sluiced across the deck for them to forge a wave. Alex took the lead, pushing the wave across the deck. Zoey flicked her fingers and the white foam at its crest opened into the gaping mouth of a shark. It swallowed crabs and snakes, washing them away from the crew and overboard.

Anil summoned a second wave. It took the shape of a charging walrus, tusks like whirlpools. The otters leaped out of its path as it careened towards the sea lion, tossing it across the deck.

"Yes!" cheered Zoey, beaming sideways at Anil.

Slowly, the tide of battle was turning in their favour. A wide, stingray-shaped wave cleared a path through the attackers.

"Push up!" Meri ordered.

"I can do a hundred!" Bridget boasted.

She and Gene ran into the space, flanked by the otters, beating back anything that had withstood the deluge.

"I think we're winning?" Anil said.

Zoey released an exhausted breath. "If anybody asks, I always thought we would."

The Water Dragon was still fighting the influence of the parasites. If they could repel the infected animals and then lend it their combined strength, there could still be a chance—

A sudden sickness doubled Alex over. Feral power plucked at the edges of his mind, a screech of mangled, jabbering sea language pounding inside his head. Zoey and Anil felt it too, staggering backwards as the baby dragon writhed inside its harness.

Beyond the battle, Callis walked calmly along the deck. Brineblood's grinning skull glared red in his hands. Oversized parasites scuttled behind him, the infected animals peeling back to let them through.

"He always shows up at the worse moments," Zoey said.

"Why are the parasites following him?" asked Anil.

"They're following Brineblood's power," Alex said, forcing himself to stand straight. "Callis is using the power of the skull to control them."

Pressing hard on the baby dragon's scales, they pushed with everything they had left. But the volatile potency of

Brineblood's skull blew a storm through their minds. Callis easily batted away the limp wave that came for him.

Bridget lunged for the pirate while Gene aimed a blow at his legs. Callis flicked a lazy hand, the skull's light flickering erratically, and summoned tendrils of water to lock around their arms and wrench them back.

"Don't let them near the dragon!" Meri bellowed.

She and Grandpa, along with the remaining crew, joined Alex, Zoey and Anil to form a barrier in front of the baby dragon. The otters bared their teeth while Kraken flared purple in warning.

Callis smiled serenely. The parasites at his back snapped their mandibles with impatience. Thousands of babies crawled across their shells, undulating like living skin.

"You've lost," Callis said. "You were never strong enough. Never deserved such a magnificent gift. The ocean respects power. The Water Dragon has been brought to heel and I will rule over it all."

Alex could sense that, above them, the Water Dragon was losing its personal battle against the regrouping parasites. Any chance of combining their power to force the monsters out was rapidly ebbing away.

"Your strength isn't real." Alex looked to the protective ring of his friends. "You're no better than a parasite."

Callis's lips twisted into a snarl and the skull blazed in his hands. An enormous wave heaved itself up beside the ship like a monster rising from the deep. The baby dragon glowed and Alex threw out a hand to try and break the water apart.

It was too strong. The wave broke over *The Dragonfly* and dashed their defensive wall to pieces. Equipment scattered and barrels overturned to spill oil across the deck and into the sea.

The parasites swarmed.

Alex washed up at the base of the rail, Kraken clinging to the side of his face. Zoey and Anil had been pushed to the other side of the ship, the others scattered here and there.

They watched in horror as the newly hatched parasites mobbed the otters, crawling over their fur in search of a way inside. The otters rolled onto their backs and twitched as the infection took hold.

More parasites teemed up the ropes of the baby dragon's harness and spread over its scales. The dragon gave a desolate cry and tried to shake them loose even as the tiny monsters found its mouth and burrowed inside.

Alex tried to hold tight to the connection between them, tried to send his strength so the baby dragon could fight.

Don't let them take over, he begged.

The baby dragon whimpered. The connection frayed like rotten rope until only a slender thread remained.

Tears streamed down Alex's face. *I'm so sorry*, he told it.

But the connection was already gone.

CHAPTER THIRTY

DEUS EX DRAGONA

Pain speared through Alex's stomach. The well of his power seemed to puncture, magic draining clear to leave him empty. The anguish of defeat bled him dry.

Everywhere, the storm intensified. *The Dragonfly* was tossed like driftwood over towering waves. Wind tore through the sails, rigging breaking loose to snap across the deck. The scattered crew held on tight to keep from being thrown overboard, but Callis, still flanked by parasites, somehow kept his feet as if glued to the planking.

The torment in Alex's belly turned molten, searing, steaming inside him like magma bubbling through the seabed. Too much for his body to contain. Surely too great to belong only to him.

Above him, the Water Dragon flung back its head and roared.

It was the sound of purest agony, the primordial rumbling of ancient fault lines shot through by the whip-crack fury of kindled lightning. *This* was the pain lancing through Alex's body. Pain strong enough to burn away the evil that blocked his connection with the dragon.

Now, he felt *everything*.

"What's happening?" Zoey had crawled beside him and shouted the words into his ear. "Are the parasites taking it over?"

Alex shook his head. The Water Dragon reached in its mind for its baby, straining to get through. When it found the connection blocked, severed by the parasites, it roared again. Lightning lashed down from the sky.

"It hasn't lost its battle with the parasites." Alex winced at a hot flash of pain. The opposite seemed to be true: the dragon's power had pushed the corruption aside, amplified by a greater purpose. "It's trying to save its baby."

One by one, the threads of the ocean lifted their voices to sing: the rhythmic cascade of the tide on pebble beaches; fluting voices of rare birds skimming the waves; heavy rain drumming on tranquil lagoons and rugged coastline.

Alex had never felt sea magic so potent; the entire ocean was being called to assemble. The waves froze in place as if holding their breath. The threads flickered and flushed with scintillating life, slow motion lightning forking through the surf. Every single one connected to the Water Dragon, the bedrock of an impossibly vast network.

"Is that...?" Anil had found his way to their side.

Alex blinked away hot tears. "You see it?"

"We see it," Zoey breathlessly confirmed.

The blazing threads left flickering trails across his vision. Tentatively, some climbed onto the deck of *The Dragonfly*, as if feeling their way through darkness. They reached for the infected animals and latched on, delving inside and flushing their bodies with light.

Slowly, glowing green specks rose from beneath their skin. Parasites plucked clear of their bodies. The otters, along with the animals that had attacked them, slumped to the deck as the infection left them.

Alex whirled around to the baby dragon. Vivid motes lifted through its scales and hovered like a constellation of stars above its body.

And then they were snuffed out.

The evicted parasites extinguished like candles thrust into the sea.

"No!" Callis howled.

The skull blazed red in his grip as he pointed to the baby dragon, sagging in its harness as it tried to recover.

The oversized parasites on deck charged towards it.

Alex and his friends tried to get to their feet, determined to protect the baby dragon. Before they could make it upright, a pulse of magic from above dropped them to their knees.

The Water Dragon roared loudly enough to split the sky. The ocean threads thrummed with power in response, growing brighter and brighter, until the entire ocean was incandescent with light. The dragon shimmered just as splendidly, as if its scales had transformed into purest magic.

Alex felt his power replenish, pouring into him so quickly it threatened to overflow. His friends gasped as the same thing happened to them. The threads were drawing magic from the dragon, every single one at once, draining every drop of power it possessed.

"Stop!" Alex shouted. "It's too much!"

The parasites charging across the deck slowed, slowed, until they came to a halt, moments from the baby dragon. Light swallowed them up and they evaporated to dust.

All across the ocean, glowing specks rose from the suspended waves, countless points of light like a luminous mist. Every parasite plucked from its blight of the water.

Simultaneously, the light began to fade from the Water Dragon's body. It drained first from its tail and left nothing behind, the proud tail fin briefly transparent before it disappeared completely.

This evaporation spread up the dragon's body, scarred armour and mosaic scales waning into empty air as the light left them.

"What's happening?" cried Zoey.

Anil sought her hand and squeezed it tight. "There won't be anything left."

"You can't go!" Alex shouted. "We need you!"

As the fade reached its neck, the Water Dragon bowed to bring its wide, ancient eyes level with Alex. The connection between them was…not dissolving. *Transforming.* Deepening into a new form he was yet to understand. The dragon half-blinked, squeezing its eyes to tell Alex it trusted him. That it could make this inevitable, irreversible metamorphosis with confidence because he was – because they were all – there to step up in its place.

"It's not leaving us," Alex told his friends. Although his voice was thick with tears, Alex found he was able to smile. "It's turning into pure sea magic. Becoming one with the ocean."

He reached for the dragon's snout. It closed its eyes in pleasure as Alex stroked its scales.

"Thank you," Alex said. "We won't let you down."

The dragon stretched its neck to nuzzle its baby, still

recovering from the excised infection. Instinctively, the baby dragon lifted its head to press against its parent.

Then the Water Dragon faded to nothing.

The threads of the ocean pulsed and the specks of light, the invasive parasites that had polluted the water, were extinguished.

The Dragonfly lurched as the sea was freed from stasis, riding a breaking wave as the storm resumed around them. The disappearing dragon left a vacuum and Brineblood's feral power rushed to fill it. It fuelled the storm, throwing it into a frenzy as the skull screeched.

Slowly, Alex climbed to his feet and turned to face Raze Callis in the middle of the deck. Shorn of his parasite army, his enemy stood defiantly with the skull of his treacherous ancestor blazing in his hands.

"It's time to finish this."

CHAPTER THIRTY-ONE

THE OCEAN KEEPS YOU

Lightning snapped at *The Dragonfly*'s mast and wind skirled through the ragged gashes in the faltering sails. Pummelling waves hurled the ship in every direction at once, pieces of the cobbled-together vessel breaking away to be snatched by the surf.

Behind Alex, the baby dragon hung listless in its harness, free of the parasites but still stunned by the powerful magic that had removed them. Strewn across the deck, reeling and sliding in the turbulence, the liberated animals were similarly dazed, shaking their stupefied heads and blinking their hazy eyes. The otters hugged each other as if they had been separated for years.

"You're on your own." Callis lifted his voice above the

wind, legs casually braced against the swaying deck. "No more Water Dragon to save you."

Hands clamped on Alex's shoulders. Zoey and Anil stepped up beside him, magic flowing freely between them.

"He's not alone," Zoey said.

"That's the difference between us." Alex plunged deep into their shared well of magic. It practically overflowed, not only replenished by the Water Dragon's transformation but reinforced, bolstered as if a dam had broken. Once, Alex had thought he was nothing without the dragon. Now the dragon had shown him the ultimate sign of trust. "Our power was a gift to wield freely. We didn't have to *steal* it."

Callis snarled. The skull in his grip blazed with ragged red light, its manic voice screaming.

"We can't control our powers well enough yet to fight him," Anil said worriedly.

"Just stick with me." Magic stronger than he'd ever felt before swirled at Alex's fingertips. "Our power is strongest together."

His friends gripped his shoulders harder.

Callis flicked a hand. A wave swiped across the deck and swatted them off their feet. Alex fell, stomach flipping, the raging water washing him and his two friends over the rail. Kraken was washed loose across the deck. The hull of *The Dragonfly* blurred past. Rough, oily waves sloshed over

Alex's head, dampening the fervour of the storm to a dull roar.

Opening an air bubble over his nose and mouth, Alex hovered briefly underwater. Zoey and Anil regrouped beside him, wearing bubbles they had given themselves.

When he surfaced, the storm bombarded his senses. Lightning licked at the crests of waves that loomed towards the sky. A sharp gust of wind thrashed him with stinging, oily spray.

Brineblood's skull possessed old dragon magic, magnified by centuries in the dragon's belly and corrupted by the old pirate's hatred and malice. It was chaotic power, driven by rage. They needed to find a way to fight it.

The light of Brineblood's skull scattered over the ocean, its delirious raving amplified by the wind, as Callis jumped up to stand on *The Dragonfly*'s railing.

The pirate flashed a shark-toothed smile. "I should probably suggest we make a deal, combine our power, and rule the ocean together."

"Yeah, all right then," Zoey said.

Callis blinked. "Really?"

"Obviously not!" Zoey scoffed. "We'd never betray the ocean."

"It might betray you," Callis said, red sparks skipping over his skin. "Now it does my bidding."

"The ocean knows you don't deserve that power," Alex shouted. "You bully it into submission. Eventually, it will reject you."

"Not if I make sure there's nobody else left who can claim its power."

"Oh yeah?" Anil shouted. "Bring it on!"

Alex was already sweeping a hand forward. Their combined magic surged. A swordfish shaped from water flew at Callis. The pirate side-stepped it, broke off its watery nose as it passed, and hurled it back at Alex like a javelin. Alex dodged and the spear whisked past his ear.

"You're going to have to do better than that." Callis smirked.

Alex thrust his hands down into the water. Seaweed rushed up from below like ravenous fish seeking food. It lashed around Callis's ankles and bound his wrists, briny tentacles trying to drag him beneath the waves.

"Yes!" cheered Anil.

"Old tricks." The skull flared and the seaweed broke like string, snapping and sinking away. "Let's try a few of your others and see how you like them."

Callis lazily spun a finger in the air. Brineblood's skull cackled. The water around Alex, Zoey and Anil began to spin, a stirring hole opening up. A vortex yawned to enclose them, spinning walls of water trapping them, tossing them helplessly around as it raged faster and faster.

"Your precious dragon caught me in a waterspout and washed me out to sea to die!" Callis roared. "When that didn't work, it had to try harder."

A guttural groan shook the waterspout apart. The stormy water was reshaping itself. A long, sinuous body, a proud head with a mighty ruff. Under Callis's command, the sea took the shape of the Water Dragon. Only its eyes were small and mean, its mouth oversized and crooked.

The twisted likeness lunged towards them, mouth opening impossibly wide, spray streaming between foamy teeth. Its jaws closed around them and they tumbled into its watery belly, dark waves thrashing, hot water scalding their skin like acid. Whenever Alex tried to open an air bubble it burst, leaving them all to choke on salt water.

Finally, the water relinquished its dragon shape and spat them out into the choppy waves. Zoey and Anil lost their grip on Alex's shoulders and floundered away.

A column of foaming water lifted from the tumult to pull up beside *The Dragonfly*. Callis stepped leisurely from the ship's rail onto its top. The water bore him smoothly down to its restless surface, where the pirate walked across the churning waves as if they were solid ground.

Lightning snapped around him from the black-bellied clouds. A deafening *WHOOSH* was followed by an intense blast of heat as the oil spilled from *The Dragonfly* sparked alight. Fire billowed across the roiling surface of the ocean. It sealed Alex and Callis inside a flaming circle, Zoey and Anil locked outside.

"Your power was always supposed to be mine," Callis said. "You've kept it from its rightful owner for too long. Finally it's passed from my ancestor to where it truly belongs. We can't allow you to pretend any longer."

The water around Alex was fierce, the fire hot against his skin, but he focused on keeping the magic inside himself calm. Surely that was the only way to defeat Brineblood's reckless power.

"If that magic truly belongs to you, throw away the skull. Let it sink to the bottom of the ocean where it belongs."

Callis snarled and tightened his grip on Brineblood's skull, fingers curling inside its empty eye sockets.

"The power belonged to *him*!" Alex called, seizing the advantage. "And he threw it away. He failed to use sea magic for what's right and used it to benefit himself instead. The Water Dragon gave me that same magic because it trusted I would use it for good. No theft. No tricks. It was a gift to me and my friends! And we will always hold it close so we can repay that trust."

The rolling light of the fire pushed wavering shadows across Callis's face. His lip curled into a snarl. "Then maybe

I'll take your bones too, when this is done."

The pirate plunged a hand into the waves. The skull cackled, sparks of power shooting along Callis's arm as he tore loose a long strip of the ocean, taking a corded whip of swirling water in his grip. Fire caught it, sweeping along the water's length.

Callis arched his arm and lashed the flaming whip at Alex. It sizzled through the air, spray puffing to steam. Alex lifted an arm across his face, focused his magic, and summoned a curved disc of water to shield himself. The whip snapped against it, scorching a piece of the shield away.

Before he could even consider a counter-attack, the whip struck again, scoring through the shield. Steam poured into the air. Alex's defence was already thinning, struggling to hold its shape against the onslaught.

Brineblood's vicious magic was too wild to resist, too potent to fight. The skull's wailing voice rampaged across the water, a relentless bombardment of babbling nonsense.

"True power belongs to whoever is strong enough to seize it!" Callis bellowed, arching his arm for a final strike. The flaming whip curved steaming over his head.

Alex dipped one last time into his well of magic. Desperation made him try and claw it to the surface, but it only drained through his fingers.

Automatically, forgetting the dragon could no longer come to his rescue, he called for help.

Please.

The storm fell suddenly quiet, although Alex could still see it raging. A familiar voice echoed inside his head. A voice that spoke the language of the ocean clearly and calmly. The same voice that had haunted him before he discovered his magic and had pushed him from strength to strength ever since. It came from all around, rippling through the water, riding on the wind and booming in every peal of thunder.

"You're here," Alex whispered.

Although he had known the Water Dragon wasn't truly gone, Alex thought it had left him, his friends and the baby dragon alone to protect the ocean. He couldn't have been more wrong. By becoming one with the single, vast power of the sea, it offered up its magic to them in its entirety. Alex's connection to the dragon now tied him more strongly than ever to the source of its power.

Alex laughed. "You're *everywhere*."

The whip sizzled through the air. Alex lifted his head and let the remains of his shield drop. Callis laughed victoriously as the flaming water found its target.

Until Alex caught the fiery whip in his hand.

Meltwater from distant glaciers coated his skin, Arctic

tides protecting his fingers from the searing heat. When Callis tried to snatch the whip back, Alex easily kept hold.

"It's time for a new way," he said.

His well of magic drew from the farthest corners of the ocean, from generations of Water Dragons who had sacrificed everything to protect it.

Pure green light swelled from Alex's hands. The fire across the waves extinguished with a hushing fizzle, banks of white steam billowing into the air. The watery whip was doused, crystals scaling along its length as it turned to solid ice. Callis's hand was trapped and the ice quickly spread over his body and down his legs.

"How are you doing this?" he bleated, as the ice encased his body, leaving just his head free. He managed to lift an arm, the skull sitting on his palm, just before he was completely frozen in place. The skull's voice mewled pitifully, red sparks bouncing harmlessly off the ice. "Let me go!" Callis pleaded.

"You were right when you said the magic doesn't belong to me." Alex stood tall. "It belongs to anybody who wants to help the world and not just themselves. It belongs to *all of us.*"

The curtain of steam was flung apart and the baby dragon swam to his side, scales blazing green. Two people clung tightly to its neck.

"Did you win without us?" Zoey asked.

Anil tutted. "Waiting for us before you strike the final blow definitely makes for a better ending."

"Except this isn't the end." Alex smiled at his friends. "It's only the beginning."

They each dropped a hand on Alex's shoulders. A current of magic flared between them. Alex pressed a hand to the baby dragon's scales and its ruff inflated.

"You can't beat me! I finally have the power!" Callis wailed. Brineblood's skull blazed and screeched, trying to break Callis free of the ice. Only now its voice was drowned out by the pure song of sea magic.

Together, Alex and his friends sent magic coursing towards Callis. The waves lifted around the encasing ice, forming the shape of hands, flippers and paws to drag Callis under.

"I'll come back!" Callis shouted. "The ocean knows me!"

Alex shook his head. "And now the ocean will keep you."

The Water Dragon had bonded with the water. It would have the strength to make sure Callis would never return to harm it ever again.

Callis's bellowing threats were silenced by ice gagging his mouth. The watery hands pulled him down and the waves closed over his head, leaving only his raised arm and Brineblood's skull above the surface. Alex heard the snap of wings and Pinch swooped past, Kraken held tightly in his grip, eight arms trailing in the air. She snatched the skull before it could sink beneath the waves, then Pinch swung back around so she could deposit it into Alex's hands.

The skull's light faded and its voice fell silent, leaving nothing but yellowed bone. But Alex still felt its terrible power tingle against his skin.

Zoey wrinkled her nose. "Holding an actual skull doesn't seem very hygienic."

"This year's Brineblood scarecrow is going to be the most realistic *ever*," Anil said.

"At least if we have the skull it can't fall into the wrong hands." Alex held it at arm's length.

"Maybe the baby dragon should swallow it," suggested Zoey. "That worked before for a few hundred years."

The baby dragon snuffed at the skull and recoiled.

"I don't think we can call it a baby any more." Alex scratched under the dragon's chin, magic dancing between them as it closed its eyes in ecstasy. "You're the Water Dragon now."

CHAPTER THIRTY-TWO

GENERATIONS OF DRAGONS

The stacked otters wobbled across the stage, whiskers and claws poking through accidental slashes in their shared costume. Kraken clung to the top for dear life, skin flushed pale except for dark spots to approximate human eyes and mouth.

"I don't walk like that," Alex said, behind the scenes. "Pretty sure I don't look like that either."

Beside him, Zoey tilted her head to one side. "I think the likeness is spot on."

At the time, it had seemed like...well, not exactly a *good* idea to cast Kraken and the otters as Alex in the play Anil had written about their adventures. It had just seemed like the best way for him to avoid performing in front of the whole town.

The stage had been built inside the boatyard, backing directly onto the sea, leaving enough space for the whole town to gather. Almost everybody had turned up.

When *The Dragonfly* had returned to Haven Bay, the harbour had been filled with tearful reunions as the rescued fishermen returned to their families. The truth of what had happened – that the Water Dragon had *not* attacked them – quickly spread.

Alex still felt a pang of sadness that so many locals had turned against the dragon. But he also understood they had been scared. He spotted Mrs Bilge in the audience, head resting on the shoulder of her grandson, and smiled.

"Now the stricken Water Dragon was finally liberated from its glass prison, true freedom lay close, yet oh so far." Anil spoke into a microphone from the side of the stage. "For Haven Bay was besieged by the rapacious ships of the dread pirate!"

"Bit melodramatic, isn't it?" Zoey said.

Alex shrugged. "You're just annoyed he wouldn't let you play yourself."

Loaf lumbered onto the stage, a long-haired wig trailing over his bulk, as the character of Zoey was announced.

The seal had been waiting for them when they returned to Haven Bay, affectionately bowling each of them over and licking their faces as they disembarked the ship. The Water

Dragon's final act, before it disappeared, had been to cure every creature of the parasites far and wide.

Onstage, Loaf exhaled a throaty burp that was definitely not in the script.

The front row of the audience – consisting of Bridget and Gene, Grandpa, Meri, Alex's dad, Mr and Mrs Wu and Mr and Mrs Chatterjee – broke into wild laughter.

"I wonder if I can sue for slander?" Zoey mused.

One face was conspicuously absent from the audience. Upon docking, Erasmus Argosy had immediately skulked back to his manor with his archive and hadn't been seen since. Despite the old man's impassioned protestations, Alex had refused to trust him with keeping Brineblood's skull. Instead, it was currently sealed in a thick glass jar under his bed while they decided how to safely dispose of its power.

The microphone squealed as Anil spoke into it too closely. "Our hero, Alex Neptune, gallantly skimmed across the waves to confront his cowardly foes."

On top of the otters, Kraken's skin shifted to approximate an angry face.

"Wielding the full might of his new-found, extraordinary powers, he joined forces with the Water Dragon to summon a prodigious storm to dash the evil ships to smithereens!"

Anil had taken more than a few liberties with the truth.

Still, Alex hoped the play would show the locals everything the dragon, as well as he and his friends, had done to protect Haven Bay and beyond. That these stories would be retold throughout the town, for years to come, updating the old legends and encouraging others to support the new dragon and fight for the ocean.

Pinch flapped over the stage, dropping pieces of debris as if the wind carried them. Zoey dipped a hand into the sea behind the stage and let a small amount of magic flow from her fingertips. Waves swelled and splashed in the background of the scene. The audience clapped in delight.

Despite their efforts to reclaim the narrative, both Zoey and Anil had asked to keep their fledgling powers secret for now. Three people in possession of powerful, legendary magic might have been harder to accept than just one. Plus, it would give them time to practise. Sharing the power with his best friends made Alex so much more confident they could live up to the Water Dragon's trust.

"Now their foe was defeated," Anil narrated, "the dragon was free to return to the waves to watch over every living thing that calls the ocean home. But not before saying goodbye to our brave heroes."

"Ready?" Alex asked.

Zoey nodded as Anil hopped down from the stage to join them. Together, they pushed their hands into the water and let their shared magic flow, a single force connecting them to every corner of the ocean.

That's your cue, Alex thought.

The waves parted and the baby dragon – no, the Water Dragon now – lifted its head above the stage, water splashing against the wood. A gasp erupted from the audience but they didn't run away like Alex had feared they might. The new story had already worked – the town was learning not to fear the dragon.

Alex took his hand from the water and climbed up onto the stage. Nerves made his knees quake. The Water Dragon lowered its head so he could stroke its muzzle. Although their connection was not yet as strong as the bond Alex had shared with its parent, it strengthened every day.

It gave him the courage to lift his voice so everybody would hear.

"The Water Dragon is our friend," he said. "It is the guardian of the ocean and will do everything it can to protect the water. But it can't do it alone."

Alex scanned the audience, meeting as many eyes as he could. The locals listened with rapt attention. His dad beamed with pride from the front row. Bridget, Grandpa and Meri nodded encouragement.

"Many stories have been told about the sea magic that the dragon and I possess," Alex continued. "There is no need to fear it. Not only because we have proved we will only use it for good. But because it is nothing compared to the power all of you have."

Now the audience murmured in confusion. Mr Ballister experimentally threw out a hand as if expecting lightning to pour from his fingers.

"You don't need magic to make a difference. Magic will never be as strong as everybody coming together to fight for what is right. No matter how powerful the Water Dragon becomes, it can't do this alone. We only stand a chance against the destructive forces that attack our ocean if *everybody* takes responsibility for protecting it."

The murmuring shifted, becoming something more resolute, people nodding to each other and standing a little taller.

The dragon's ruff inflated and its scales glowed glorious green. Magic sang along their bond, through the connections Alex shared with his friends and the gathered sea creatures. He wondered if anybody in the audience heard it too.

"We still have so much to learn," Alex said. The dragon was so young, so small. It almost felt wrong to send it out to sea by itself. Except it wouldn't truly be alone. "We're strong together. We're the new generation of dragons."

Satisfaction grumbled in the Water Dragon's throat as it nuzzled his hand.

"Go on," Alex said. "We'll see you soon."

The Water Dragon ducked away beneath the waves, splashing them playfully as its powerful tail fin propelled it across Haven Bay. As they watched it swim away, a member of the audience began to clap. Another joined in, and another, applause spreading across the crowd until the whole town was clapping.

"Do you think the play went okay?" Anil asked, appearing beside him.

Zoey scoffed. "It was terrible. I loved it." She looked to Alex. "Do you think the dragon – the last one, I mean – would have liked it?"

As Alex watched the water, a wave swelled unusually high against the flow of the tide, kicking a haze of spray into the air. The sun shone through it and cast a vivid rainbow over the sea.

Alex smiled. "I know it did."

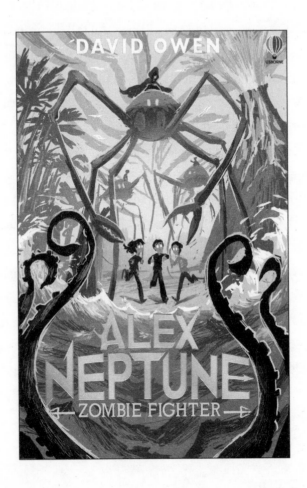

THERE ARE MORE OCEAN-SIZED ADVENTURES TO COME IN

ALEX NEPTUNE
ZOMBIE FIGHTER

When an ominous sea fog rolls in to Haven Bay,
Alex, Zoey and Anil are ambushed by mysterious
crab-legged creatures, who seem to be searching
for Brineblood's skull.
Trapped in Argosy Manor, the friends must enter
three perilous bottle-worlds and track down the
prongs of a magic trident to stop Brineblood's
zombie army – all without dying horribly in
the process...

READ ON FOR A SNEAK PEEK...

The fog smothered Haven Bay, a thick blanket of grey vapour that draped itself across the cobbled streets and banked up against the shopfronts like fresh blown snow. Alex waded through it, clothes growing damp and seeming to drag him back. Zoey and Anil stuck close to his elbows, the otters scurrying around their ankles.

It was impossible to tell where the scream had come from. An attack could be happening right in front of them and they wouldn't know.

"It's like being inside a cloud," Anil said, physically trying to push the fog apart with his arms.

Zoey sneezed. "Or going into the bathroom after my dad's sprayed deodorant."

Alex lifted an arm ahead of himself as he hurried along the street. The fog always rolled in from the sea, which meant at least some of it was made from ocean water. There were no threads for him to grasp, but Alex let his magic flow regardless. It seeped uncertainly from his fingers to search for a connection. That other magic, cold and fierce, seethed within the fog, pouncing to snuff his power out.

A faint shape darted through the cloying mist, slipping into the veiled space between buildings.

"Did you see...?"

Alex's foot caught on something and he fell sprawling

onto the cobbles. He'd tripped on a body, lying in the road.

"The monstha isth back!"

The body moved, weakly trying to fight Alex off. Alex sat up to find a crowd standing over him. He recognized his dad, along with Mr and Mrs Chatterjee and Mr and Mrs Wu. They were tending to Mr Ballister, a local man, who lay on the cobbles beside him.

"Is everything okay?" Alex asked.

The old man was wide-eyed and pointed all around them. "A pferrible monstha! Athacked me in the thog!"

"Has anybody seen his teeth?" Mrs Chatterjee asked.

A seagull hopped out of the fog, a pair of false teeth clenched in his beak, and dropped them at Anil's feet.

"Thanks, Pinch!" Anil patted his pet seagull, who could always be relied on to retrieve a lost item whether its owner wanted it back or not. He rubbed the teeth clean on his trousers and shoved them back into Mr Ballister's mouth.

"A terrible monster!" the old man immediately roared more clearly. "It ambushed me from this terrible miasma, teeth gnashing, trying to eat my brains!"

"Wouldn't have been much of a meal," Zoey muttered.

"We heard your high-pitched scream and came as quickly as we could," Alex said.

Mr Ballister cleared his throat and replied in a deeper voice than usual. "That must have been somebody else."

Footsteps clattered across the cobbles towards them. Zoey spun around, ready to fight, but dropped her fists when Bridget Neptune, Alex's sister, and her friend Gene Lennox emerged from the fog.

"We couldn't find anything," Bridget said.

Despite the chill of the fog, she wore a brightly sequined vest top that showed off her muscular arms and shoulders. Beside her, despite being swamped in an enormous hoodie, Gene looked half her size.

Alex squinted through the dense fog and realized they were standing in the town square. The concrete bowl of the fountain was a vague lump in the mist. Alex wondered why he hadn't heard the sound of its jets. Moving closer, he found the water in the fountain was frozen, its stream turned to ice in mid-air.

"It's not that cold," he said, even as a shiver slid like an icicle down his back.

Zoey rounded on Mr Ballister. "Tell us exactly what you saw."

Mr Ballister allowed the group to help him to his feet. "Death scuttling on a thousand legs," he intoned. "Frost transfigured into rotten flesh!"

"Cool, but not terribly helpful." Anil scribbled down some notes.

"We'll take him home and make sure he's all right," said

Mr Chatterjee. Anil's parents were doctors at the local hospital.

"I'll go with you to keep you safe." Anil puffed up proudly. "Call me on the walkie-talkies if you find anything."

He joined his parents in leading Mr Ballister away, the otters trotting after them as extra protection. They passed Grandpa finally catching up, breathing hard.

"What did I miss?"

"Monsters, mystery, old men being unhelpful," Zoey summarized. "The usual."

"He might have just seen somebody else in the fog and mistaken them for a monster," Alex said. "Maybe he just slipped and hurt himself."

Anil frowned at his notes. "He did seem genuinely scared."

Unfortunately, Haven Bay was the kind of place where the most improbable explanation was also usually the right one.

"Let's patrol," Alex said. "Two groups, so we can cover more ground."

Alex joined Bridget, Gene and his dad, while Zoey teamed up with her parents and Grandpa. Zoey handed him a walkie-talkie.

"Remember the emergency code words?" she asked.

Alex sighed. "Sadly, yes."

"Then stay gelid and toast a flare if you dredge up any chum."

Alex nodded – despite having no idea what she'd said – and accepted a seafire lantern. The green liquid mixed from phosphorescent ocean algae glowed brightly, the light of its cold fire pressing back against the fog.

The two groups left the square from opposite sides and ventured into the murk.

"Do you think he actually saw something?" Gene asked.

"If he did, it'll think twice before it messes with me." Bridget rolled her hulking shoulders to limber up.

The empty streets quickly silenced her bravado. Over the last few weeks, nobody else had dared to be outside after dark. The library and the Chipping Forecast chip shop were locked up tight with no lights on inside. The fog seemed to both dampen and amplify noises. Their footsteps on the cobbles barely made a sound, while water dripping from a gutter sounded like cannon shots striking the street.

They ended up walking in a shrinking huddle without even realizing it.

"Can't you magic away the fog or something?" Alex's dad asked.

It had taken a while to convince his dad about sea magic and the responsibility it placed on Alex's shoulders. Even though he accepted it now, it was not so easy to make him understand how it worked.

"I tried, the first night it hit the town," Alex replied.

He hadn't been able to get any kind of grip on the fog, no matter how hard he pushed his magic. It was the same for Zoey and Anil. That other power, similar to their own but also different, held the fog stubbornly in place.

They just needed to discover what it was being used to hide.

A wet slurping noise rasped from somewhere nearby. The group froze, Alex lifting the seafire lantern higher. Its green glow reflected from the fog instead of breaking through it.

"What is it?" asked Alex's dad, voice trembling.

A final slurp was followed by a bass rumble, a deep-throated growl, before slapping footsteps advanced towards them.

Slap, slap.

"Get behind me." Bridget stepped in front of the group.

Slap, slap.

A low, round shape lumbered from the murk. Alex reached for his well of magic, despite being unsure if he'd be able to use it.

Loaf, an incredibly round harbour seal, shuffled from the gloom and belched.

"So it *is* a horrible monster," Bridget concluded.

Alex sagged with relief, realizing only now how hard his heart was hammering in his chest. He leaned down to scratch the seal's ears. He had faced monsters before – thousands of them, in fact, ocean parasites the size of dogs. But it was a more frightening prospect to encounter a monster so close to home rather than out at sea, where it would be harder to keep the town and its people safe.

Maybe Mr Ballister had glimpsed Loaf in the fog and mistaken him for some fiend. Maybe there was nothing frightening—

Alex cut off the thought, remembering Anil's oft-repeated warning: never tempt fate.

Their walkie-talkie fuzzed. Alex winced. Too late.

"*I just spotted something.*" Anil's voice, laced with fear.

"*Code red, yellow or aquamarine?*" Zoey asked.

"*Uh, orange? It was too big to be a person. It was heading west across the town square.*"

Alex glanced nervously at his group. That was the direction they had taken and they hadn't travelled far.

"We're just past the library," Gene reported into the walkie-talkie.

"*Roger that.*" Zoey's voice fuzzed as she took a sharp breath. "*I see it. Chum on the wing! Radar ping west by south-west, scudding smooth on collision course!*"

Alex grabbed the walkie-talkie. "I don't know what any of that means!"

"*It's coming straight for you!*"

Before he could respond, the fog swirled and Alex was knocked off his feet as a monster pounced from the gloom.

To find out what happens next,
look out for

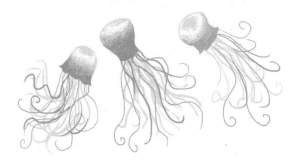

ACKNOWLEDGEMENTS

It's a threequel! A trilogy! A triumvirate! Yes, there are now three of these stupid books, and I wouldn't have got this far without lots of people.

As ever, enormous thanks to the Usborne team and everybody who worked on this book and the series so far: Sarah, Anne, Jacob, Jess, Fritha, George, Will, Sarah, Hannah, and whoever else I'm no doubt forgetting. You've all made this series more successful than I ever dreamed.

Ella, my agent, who is hugely dedicated and passionate about her job and my work. I can't believe we've been working together for 10 years!

Sarah, for her love and support, expert writing expertise, and love of the weirdest ideas possible. I did my best to out-weird her books with this one but I don't think I quite managed it.

Darran, to whom this book is dedicated, not only because he continues to humour my obscure aquatic questions, but also for his continued support and enthusiasm for my "*Die Hard* inside a kaiju" story idea. I actually got to write it!

Maisie and Leila once again offered thoughtful and insightful sensitivity reads. This is invaluable work done only to improve books, to make them kinder and more inclusive, and yet it is under attack from people with a hateful agenda. I couldn't be prouder or more grateful to have sensitivity reads of my work.

Lastly, thank you to all the booksellers, librarians, teachers, parents and others who have supported this series. Seeing it in the hands of young readers is the best feeling in the world.